CLEAN SWEEP

CLEAN SWEEP

ILONA ANDREWS

ISBN-13: 9781494388584

Acknowledgments

We started CLEAN SWEEP as a fun, for-the-love project. Every week we'd write a little bit and post the first draft online and readers would get to comment on it. It was almost like writing in front of an audience. The hardest challenge was the story itself. In a normal novel, you can go back and rewrite the scenes. The format of CLEAN SWEEP meant there would be no second chances. Once something was posted, it was there to stay.

It is very rare when an author gets to interact with their audience to that extent. Writing Clean Sweep was a very educational experience for us. We were fortunate enough to get your input on the story as it unfolded and we feel privileged that so many of you chose to read it and comment. Your contributions and comments made the story so much better and we're are deeply grateful to all of you. There are a few people to whom we would like to extend especial thanks.

Doris Mantair for her incredible art. You can find out more about Doris at disanthus.com.

Anne Victory for her copyedit. You can find more about Anne at her website: victoryediting.com.

Beta Readers for their efforts to make this manuscript the best it could be: Julie Heckert, Shannon Daigle, William Stonier, Erin Oleski, Bethany Geleskie, Neal Bravin, Christian, Mary Roark, Denise Gray, Sarah Gibson, Katelin

Campbell, Areerat Dallimore, Ruth Hardaway, Victoria, Milly Ward, and others.

As always, all errors of fact and grammar are our fault entirely. We hope you will join us again for the sequel to Clean Sweep starting early in 2014. We'll post in the same place, demo.ilona-andrews.com

CHAPTER ONE

Brutus was dead. His body lay under an oak on the Hendersons' lawn. A small group of neighbors had gathered around his corpse, their faces sad and shocked.

It had been such a nice morning. The Texas summer had finally cooled a little, allowing for a light, happy breeze. Not a single cloud marked the blue sky, and the walk to the twenty-four-hour gas-station convenience store had turned out to be downright pleasant. Normally I didn't go shopping at the gas station at seven thirty on Friday morning, but when you run a bed-and-breakfast, it's a good policy to accommodate requests from your guests, especially if they've paid for a lifetime membership. So I gathered my blond hair in a ponytail, put on my flowered skirt and a pair of sandals, and hightailed it half a mile to the store.

I was coming back, carrying my purchases, when I saw my neighbors gathered under the tree. And just like that, my happy day ground to a halt.

"Hey, Dina," Margaret Pineda said.

"Hello." I glanced at the body. A second's worth of looking told me everything I needed to know. Just like the other two.

Brutus hadn't been what you would call a good dog. An oversized black Chow Chow, he'd been suspicious of everyone, ornery, and often too loud for his own good. His chief activity when he'd managed to escape Mr. Byrne's yard had been hiding behind trash cans and exploding with thunderous barking at anyone who dared to walk by. But no matter how annoying he'd been, he hadn't deserved to die.

No dog deserved to die this way.

"Maybe it's a mountain lion," Margaret said. Tan, slight, with a fluffy cloud of dark, curly hair framing her face, Margaret was in her mid-forties. She looked at the body again and turned away, her fingers covering her mouth. "That's just terrible."

"Like, a real mountain lion?" Kayley Henderson raised her head from her phone. Being seventeen, Kayley lived for drama.

David Henderson shrugged his shoulders. He was a heavy man, not fat, but thick around the middle. He and his wife owned a pool-supplies shop in town and did their best to parent Kayley, with mixed success.

"Here? In a subdivision?" David shook his head.

"Why not?" Margaret crossed her arms. "We've got owls."

"Owls fly," David pointed out.

"Well, of course they fly. They're birds."

It hadn't been a mountain lion. A puma would've pinned the dog and bitten through the nape of his neck, then dragged him off or at least eaten the stomach and the insides. The thing that had killed Brutus had smashed his skull with a devastating blow. Then it had scoured the dog's sides and sliced open its abdomen, releasing the intestines, but hadn't taken a single bite. This was a territorial kill, left for everyone to find —*look how bad and clever I am.*

"That's the third dog in two weeks," Margaret said. "It has to be a mountain lion."

The first had been a lovable but dumb escape-artist boxer one street over. She'd been found the exact same way, disemboweled, behind the hedge by the mailboxes. The second had been a beagle named Thompson, a notorious lawn bandit who'd made it his life's mission to add a present to every patch of mowed grass. He'd been left in the shadow of a shrub. And now Brutus.

Brutus had a lot of fur. Whatever had made those gashes in his sides had to have long claws. Long, razor-sharp, and growing from fingers with a lot of manual dexterity.

"What do you think, Dina?" Margaret asked.

"Oh, it's a mountain lion," I said. "Definitely."

David exhaled through his nose. "I'm done with this. I've got to take Kayley to school and open the store in fifteen minutes. Did anyone call Byrne?"

Brutus was Mr. Byrne's pride and joy. He'd walk him every afternoon through the subdivision, beaming when people stopped to pay him compliments.

"I did," Margaret told him. "He must've gone to take his grandkids to school. I left a message."

Hi, I'm so sorry to tell you your dog died in a horrible way... It had to stop. Now.

A man strode up the street. He walked with a light spring in his step that said he could run and run very fast if he chose. Sean Evans. Just the devil I wanted to see.

Sean Evans was a new addition to Avalon Subdivision. Rumor said he was ex-military. The rumor was probably right. In my experience, the ex-military guys came in two types. The first grew long hair, sprouted beards, and indulged in all the things they hadn't been able do while they'd been in the armed forces. The second did their best to pretend they never got out.

Sean Evans belonged to the second category. His russet-brown hair was cut short. His square jaw was clean-shaven. Tall and broad-shouldered, he had a strong, fit body, honed by exercise to a lean, muscular precision. He looked like he could pick up a fifty-pound rucksack, run across the city with it, and then beat an ungodly number of enemies to a bloody pulp with his bare hands while things exploded dramatically in the background. He was said to be unfailingly polite, but something in his stare communicated a clear "don't mess with me" message.

"Sean!" Margaret waved. "We've got another dead dog!"

Sean made a slight adjustment to his course, heading straight for us.

"He's so hot it's sick," Kayley volunteered.

David turned purple in the face. "The man's twenty-seven years old. That's too old for you."

"I didn't say I wanted to date him, Dad. Jeez."

For me hotness was a complicated matter involving brains, humor, and some other things, but all that aside, I was willing to admit Sean Evans was nice to look at. Unfortunately, in light of the events two nights ago, he was also the prime suspect for the dog killings.

Sean stopped and looked at Brutus. As he glanced up, I checked his eyes. They were amber, a particular shade of brown with a touch of a golden hue, almost orange in the sunlight, and they were surprised. He hadn't killed Brutus. I let out a quiet breath.

A black SUV pulled around the bend. Mr. Byrne. Oh no.

The Hendersons beat a strategic retreat while Margaret waved at the SUV. Sean looked at the dog some more, shook his head, and sidestepped the body. He was about to take off. Stopping him and catching his attention was a terrible idea. Getting involved in this whole dead-dog affair in any way was an even worse idea. But the alternative was to do nothing. I'd done nothing the first two times, and the serial murderer of the dogs showed no signs of stopping.

"Mr. Evans?" I called. "A moment of your time?"

He looked at me as if he'd never seen me before. "Do I know you?"

"My name is Dina. I own the bed-and-breakfast."

He glanced past me at the old house sitting at the mouth of the subdivision. "That monstrosity?"

Aren't you sweet? "Yes."

"What can I do for you?"

In the street, the SUV screeched to a halt. Mr. Byrne stepped out. A short, older man, he seemed to shrink even more as he approached his dog's body. His face had gone white as a sheet. Both Sean and I looked at him for a brief second.

"How long do you intend to let this continue?" I asked quietly.

Sean frowned. "I don't follow."

"Something is obviously killing dogs in your territory. One would think you would want to take care of that."

Sean fixed me with a thousand-yard stare. "Ma'am, I don't know what the hell you're talking about."

Ma'am? *Ma'am?* I was at least four years younger than him.

Mr. Byrne knelt on the grass by Brutus's body. His face went slack.

"The first two dogs were hidden, but this one is in plain view. Whatever is killing them is escalating, and it's taunting you. It's leaving its kill where everyone can see."

Sean's face gained a no-nonsense-tolerated expression. "I think you might be crazy."

Mr. Byrne looked ready to topple over.

"Excuse me." I set my grocery bag on the grass, walked around Sean, and crouched by the older man. He put his hand over his face.

5

"I'm so sorry."

"I don't understand," Mr. Byrne said, his voice hollow. "He was fine this morning when I let him out in the yard. I don't understand... How did he even get out?"

Margaret decided it was a good moment to escape and backed away.

"Why don't you go back to the house?" I said. "I'll get my car and bring Brutus to you."

His hand was shaking. "No, he's my dog. I've got to take him to the vet..."

"I'll help you," I promised.

"I'll get something to line the trunk with," Sean said. "Give me a minute."

"I can't..." Mr. Byrne's face stiffened.

"I'll take care of it," Sean said. "I'm sorry for your loss."

Sean returned with some clear garden plastic. It took about five minutes for us to wrap Brutus' remains and Sean carried the bundle into the back of the SUV. Mr. Byrne got in, and Sean and I watched the vehicle take off.

"I just want to avoid any misunderstandings," I said. "Since you refuse to defend your territory, I'll have to take care of it."

He leaned closer to me. "Lady, I thought I told you already –I don't know what you're talking about. Go back to your place and sweep the porch or whatever it is you do up there."

He wanted to pretend to be dense. There wasn't much I could do about that. Maybe he was a coward, although he didn't seem the type. Maybe he just didn't care. Well, I cared. It would have to be enough.

"Very well. As long as you don't get in my way, we won't have a problem. So nice to meet you, Mr. Evans."

I started up the street toward my house.

"Lady, you're crazy!" he called after me.

I might be crazy, but I was very rarely wrong, and I had a strong feeling that life in the suburbs of Red Deer, Texas, had just gotten a lot more complicated.

The Gertrude Hunt Bed-and-Breakfast sat at the entrance of the Avalon Subdivision, on three acres of land, most of it taken up by the orchard and garden. Several mature oaks shaded the house, and a four foot hedge bordered the lawn along the side facing the street. The building's original fish-scale wood siding had long rotted away and been replaced by a more practical, modern version in deep hunter green. Built in the late 1880s, the three-story inn had all the over-wrought American Queen Anne features: a deep wrap-around porch with short Corinthian columns guarding the entrance, three small second-story balconies, overhanging eaves, and both bay and oriel windows projecting seemingly in random places. Like many of the older Victorian houses, the inn was asymmetric, and if one looked at it from the north side and then from the south, it wouldn't even look like the same house. Its eastern wall featured a small tower; its western side sported a round, protruding sunroom. It was as if a medieval castle and a Southern-belle, antebellum mansion had a baby and it had been delivered into the world by a gothic wedding-cake decorator.

The inn was lavished with spindle-work, didn't make sense, and was too elaborate, but it wasn't a monstrosity.

I walked up the porch stairs and petted the pale column. "He's a rude idiot. Don't pay him any attention. I think you're charming."

The house didn't answer.

I stepped inside and my heart made a quiet little leap in my chest as I nodded at the photograph of my parents hanging in the front room. Every time I went out, some small part of me hoped that when I came back, I would find them right there in the hallway, waiting for me.

I swallowed, turned left, climbed up the spacious staircase to the second floor, and came out onto the north balcony where Her Grace Caldenia ka ret Magren was taking her tea. She looked to be in her mid-sixties, but it was the kind of sixties one achieved after living for years in the lap of luxury. Her platinum-gray hair was pulled back from her face into a smooth knot. She had a strong profile with a classic Greek nose, pronounced cheekbones, and blue eyes that usually had a slightly forlorn look unless she found something funny. She held her teacup with utmost elegance, gazing down at the street with a slightly sardonic, melancholy demeanor.

I hid a smile. Caldenia was worldly, wise, and fashionably weary of life. Despite her detached air, she had no intentions of going gently into that good night and had gone to a great length to make sure she wouldn't pass on any time soon.

I opened the plastic shopping bag and pulled out a yellow plastic package and a yellow can. "Your Funyuns and Mello Yello, Your Grace."

"Ah!" Caldenia came to life. "Thank you."

She opened the bag with a flick of her fingers and shook a few Funyun rings onto a plate. Her long fingers plucked one up, and she bit into it and chewed with obvious pleasure.

"How did it go with the werewolf?" she asked.

I sat in the chair. "He's pretending I'm insane and that he doesn't know what I'm talking about."

"Perhaps he's repressed."

I raised my eyebrows.

Caldenia delicately chewed another Funyun. "Some of them do mentally castrate themselves in that way, dear. Controlling, religious mother; weak, passive father –you know how it goes. Genetic memory does have its limits. Personally, I was never one for denying your urges."

Yes, and several million people had paid the price.

Caldenia placed her thumbnail against the rim of the Mello Yello can and turned it. The metal squeaked. She popped the tab and neatly lifted the top off of the can. The edge of the cut was razor-sharp. She poured the contents into her teacup and drank, smiling.

"He's not repressed," I said. "He's spent the last two months marking every inch of what he considers his territory."

Caldenia raised her eyebrows. "You saw him?"

I nodded. Even in the dark Sean Evans was difficult to mistake for anyone else. It was the way he moved –a supple, powerful predator on the prowl.

"Did you get a glimpse of his equipment?"

"Honestly, now..."

Caldenia shrugged. "I just want to know if it's ample. A natural curiosity."

Sure, curiosity. "I have no idea. He was relatively modest about it and I didn't linger."

"There is your mistake." Caldenia sipped her tea. "*Carpe diem quam minimum credula postero*, my dear."

"I'm not interested in seizing any of Sean Evans' days. I just want him to stop the dog murderer."

"None of this is your problem, you know. The inn hasn't been threatened."

"These people are my neighbors." *Yours, too.* "They have no idea what they're dealing with. The killer is getting bolder. What if it kills a child next?"

Caldenia rolled her eyes. "Then whatever passes for law enforcement in this corner of the universe will deal with it. They will likely spectacularly fail, but the perpetrator either will stop to avoid attracting any more attention or perhaps the Senate will send someone to deal with it. Either way, my dear, not your problem."

I looked down the street. From the balcony I could see nearly three hundred yards down to the first bend of the ridiculously named Camelot Road before it curved this way and that through the subdivision. People hurried to work. To the right a couple of toddlers rode their tricycles up and down the concrete driveway in front of their house. To the left Margaret was refilling her bird feeder while a small, fluffy ball of reddish fur that was supposedly a Pomeranian bounced up and down at her feet.

They were my neighbors. They had their normal lives and ordinary problems. They lived in the suburbs, struggled with debt and a faltering economy, and tried to save for their children's college. Most of them weren't equipped to deal with things that had sharp teeth and a predatory intelligence stalking them in the night. Most of them didn't even know things like that existed.

My imagination conjured something with long claws bursting from under the hedges and snatching up a toddler. The rules and laws by which I lived said I shouldn't get involved. I was neutral by definition, which gave me certain protections, and once I compromised that neutrality, I'd be fair game for whatever owned those claws.

"Misha!" Margaret called.

The Pomeranian dashed around her, all but flying over green grass.

"Misha! Come here, you little brat!"

Misha dashed the other way, thoroughly enjoying the game. In a minute Margaret would lose her patience and chase her.

You'd have to be a heartless snake to leave them to deal with a monster on their own. Caldenia, despite her twin hearts, was quite heartless, but it didn't mean I had to be.

Caldenia crunched another Funyun.

I smiled. "More Mello Yello, Your Grace?"

"Yes, please."

I fished another can out of the bag. There would be no more dead dogs if I could help it.

I opened my eyes. My bedroom lay shrouded in gloom, the moonlight painting long silvery stripes on the old wooden floor. The magic chimed in my head. Something had crossed the boundary of the inn's grounds. Well, something magically active or weighing more than fifty pounds. The inn was pretty good at distinguishing between a potential threat and random wildlife that wandered onto the grounds.

I sat up. Next to the bed, Beast raised her tiny head from her dog bed.

I listened. Crickets chirped. A cool breeze drifted through the screen of the open window, stirring the beige curtains. The wooden floor felt cool under my bare feet. I really should get a rug in here.

Another gentle chime. It felt as if someone had tossed a rock into calm water and the ripples splashed against my skin. Definitely an intruder.

I stood up. Beast made a mad lunge and licked my ankle. I took the broom from its spot against the wall and left the bedroom. A long hallway stretched before me, dappled with cool darkness and moonlight coming through the large bay windows. I walked along the hallway, zeroing in on the disturbance. The Shih Tzu trotted next to me like a vigilant seven-pound black-and-white mop.

The inn and I were bound so tightly it was almost an extension of me. I could target any intrusion with pinpoint accuracy. This particular intruder wasn't moving. He was milling about in one spot.

The house was dark and quiet around me. I crossed the hallway, turned, and stopped at a door to the western balcony. Something moved below, in the orchard. Let's see what the night dragged in. Soundlessly, the door swung open in front of me, and I stepped out onto the balcony.

In the orchard, twenty yards from the house, Sean Evans was urinating on my apple tree.

You've got to be kidding me.

"Stop that," I hissed in a theatrical whisper.

He ignored me. His back was to me and he was still wearing the same jeans and gray T-shirt I'd seen him in that morning.

"Sean Evans! I see you. Stop marking your territory on my apple tree."

"Don't worry," he said without turning. "It won't hurt the apples."

The nerve. "How would you know? You've probably never grown an apple tree in your entire life."

"You wanted me to handle it," he said. "I'm handling it."

He was handling it, all right. "What makes you think that marking things will have any effect? The dog killer ignored your marks before."

"This is how it's done," he said. "There is a certain etiquette to these things. He challenged me, and now I'll challenge him back."

"Not in my orchard, you won't. Get out."

Beast barked once to add her support.

"What is that?" he asked.

"It's a dog."

Sean zipped himself up, turned around, and took a running start at an oak tree. It was an incredible thing to watch: six feet away from the oak he leapt up and forward, bounced off the bark upward to the spot where two large branches split from the trunk, pushed off them like he was weightless, landed on the branch stretching toward the balcony, ran along it until it thinned, and crouched. The whole thing took less than two seconds.

His eyes shone once with bright golden amber. His face had gained a dangerous sharpness, predatory and slightly feral. A shiver ran down my spine. No, not repressed. Not even a little bit.

A werewolf was bad news. Always. If I had met him on the street like this, I'd have started making soothing noises and thinking of exit strategies. But we were on my turf.

"That's not a dog," Sean said.

Beast let out a tiny snarl, astonished at the insult.

"She weighs what, about six, seven pounds? Now, I'm willing to concede that somewhere in the distant past one of her ancestors might have been a dog. But now she's an oversized chinchilla."

"First you insult my house, now you insult my dog." I leaned on my broom.

"She has little ponytails," Sean said, nodding at the two tiny ponytails above the Shih Tzu's eyes.

"Her fur gets in her eyes. She's due for a grooming."

"Aha." Sean tilted his head to the side. He seemed completely feral now. "You're asking me to take a dog with two ponytails seriously."

"I'm not asking you to do anything. I'm telling you: get off my property."

He bared his teeth at me in a slightly deranged smile. He looked hungry. "Or what? You'll hit me with your broom?"

Something like that. "Yes."

"I'm so scared right now I'm practically shaking."

He was within the inn's boundary. I was clearly an inn-keeper —the broom was a dead giveaway. Yet he showed no respect. I'd met some arrogant werewolves —when you were a highly effective killing machine, you tended to think the world was your oyster —but this one took the cake. "Go away, *siri.*" There. That would fix him.

"Name's Sean." He tilted his head again.

No reaction to the insult. Either he had a bulletproof ego or he had no idea I'd just called him a sniveling coward in his own language.

Sean tilted his head. "So how does a girl like you know about werewolves?"

"A girl like me?"

"How old are you?"

"Twenty-four."

"Most twenty-four-year-old women I know sleep in some-thing more revealing. Something more adult."

I raised my eyebrows. "There is nothing wrong with my Hello Kitty T-shirt." It was thin and comfortable, and it reached to my mid-thigh, which meant that if I had to get up in the middle of the night to dispatch any intruders, I'd do it with my butt covered and modesty intact.

Sean frowned. "Sure, if you're five. Got a touch of arrested development happening there?"

Argh. "What I have happening is none of your business."

"It fits," he said.

"What?"

"The T-shirt. It fits your whole lifestyle. I bet you grew up around here too."

Where was he going with this? "Maybe."

"Probably never left the town, right? Never been any-where, never done anything crazy, and now you run this bed-and-breakfast and drink tea with old ladies on a bal-cony. A nice quiet life."

Ha! "There is nothing wrong with a nice quiet life."

"Sure." Sean shrugged. "When I was twenty-four, I wanted to see the world. I wanted to go places and meet people."

I couldn't resist. "And kill them."

He bared his teeth at me. "Sometimes. The point is, if you've stayed around here all your life, how do you know about werewolves? There isn't one for miles, and if there is, they're dormant. I combed this territory before I took it. The closest werewolf is in a suburb of Houston, and when I spoke to him, he confirmed that there hasn't been an active werewolf in this area for years. So how do you know about werewolves?"

"Don't like your own kind much, do you?"

"Do you always duck the questions or am I just special?"

"You're special," I told him, sinking as much sarcasm into it as I could. "Now shoo. Go on."

He dipped his head and stared at me, with unblinking, focused intensity like a wolf in the middle of winter sighting his prey. His eyes shone, catching the moonlight. Every hair on the back of my neck rose.

"I'll find out. I don't like being out of the loop."

And now he was threatening me. That does it. One more word and he'd regret ever opening his mouth. "Leave. Now."

The werewolf grinned at me, his eyes full of wild. "Fine, fine. Sleep tight."

He dropped off the branch, fell two stories to the ground, landed in a soft half crouch, and took off running.

His long legs carried him out of my orchard, and a second later the magic chimed in my head, announcing that he had left the inn grounds.

I turned and walked back to my bedroom, the balcony door closing softly behind me. Obnoxious smart-ass. Never been anywhere, never done anything, huh. Arrested development, huh. Considering that it was coming from a man who spent his nights peeing on his neighbors' fences, that was rich. Shoot, I should've told him that. Oh well, too late now.

I climbed back into bed. They didn't call his kind lunatics for nothing. At least he decided to do something about the dog killer.

Half an hour later I decided it was time to stop thinking up witty and inventive insults involving werewolves. The house was quiet. Beast snored softly. I yawned, flipped over my warm pillow, and scooted deeper under the covers. Time to go to sleep...

The magic rippled, splashing against me like a tide. Someone was running along the edge of the inn's grounds, skimming it. It was moving fast, too fast for a human. It could be Sean, but somehow I doubted it.

CHAPTER TWO

I knelt by the spot where the intruder had veered off from the inn's boundary. Four triangular indentations marked the hard soil –claw marks. The trespasser had sunk its claws into the ground as it turned on its foot and dashed off. I had just missed it.

In front of me the street lay silent, the trees mere charcoal shadows rustling softly in the wind like sheets of paper sliding against each other. The subdivision was hardly rambunctious, and even on Friday nights, the activity died down by midnight. It was close to one o'clock.

I breathed in quietly, listening, watching. No hint of movement anywhere. No stray noises. I'd taken three precious seconds to throw on some shorts and a thicker T-shirt and snap a rubber band around my hair, and now the thing with claws was gone.

I raised my hand, focused my power on the tips of my fingers, and then touched the indentation. A pale yellow trail ignited on the ground. It faded almost instantly, but not before I registered its direction. It was heading down the street, deeper into the subdivision.

Chasing it would mean leaving the inn's grounds, where I was at my strongest. I should stay out of it. I should turn around and go back to bed. It was none of my business.

If it killed a child, I wouldn't be able to live with myself. I'd made my decision, for better or worse. Now wasn't the time to have doubts.

I needed a weapon. Something with reach. I concentrated. The broom flowed in my hand, the "plastic" of its handle melting into dark metal shot through with hairline fractures of glowing, brilliant blue. A razor-sharp blade formed on one end while the shaft of the broom elongated to seven feet. An old line from an Italian martial-arts manual popped into my head: the longer the spear, the less deceiving it is. Seven feet would do.

The last of the blue cracks melted. The spear, now the dark gray of Teflon, felt comforting in my hand. I took off down the road, keeping to the shadows. The glowing trail faded. I would've loved to rekindle it, but I'd left the inn's grounds and my bag of fun tricks had shrunk.

Avalon Subdivision had been built by a drunkard who couldn't draw a straight line if his life had depended on it. The streets didn't just turn, they curved and looped back on themselves as if they were the whorls of a giant's thumbprint. Camelot Road was the subdivision's main street, and even it bent like a snake slithering through the forest of houses. I passed by the side streets, briefly glancing down each one. Gawain Street, Igraine Road, Merlin Circle… The streets lay empty. Here and there lights were still on, but most of the residents had gone to bed.

Galahad Road.

A floodlight shone bright in the distance. Probably motion triggered. Someone or something was moving outside.

Keep going or check it out? If it was nothing, it would cost me time. But if it was something, I could stop looking.

I crossed the street to the opposite side and ran, hiding in the shadows of mature oaks. It would only take a minute.

A house sat in the shadow of a poplar tree. Gray Texas limestone, two stories, bay window, two-car garage –pretty standard fare for the subdivision. A car sat in the driveway, a Honda Odyssey, both passenger doors and the hatch open, showing white plastic bags in the cargo area, probably from a twenty-four-hour grocery store. The familiar shape of a child's car seat curved in the back. The door of the house stood ajar.

A couple coming home from a trip, maybe? They must've stopped at the store on the way so they wouldn't have to go out tomorrow, come home, parked, and taken their child inside. It was probably nothing, but I wouldn't know until I took a closer look.

The house directly across the street from the limestone offered no cover, but the property right before it had a nice thick hedge. I snuck over to the hedge and crouched to the side of it, resting my spear in the grass.

A car started somewhere deeper in the subdivision and drove away, the sound of its engine fading. Silence claimed the night. The moon shone bright, a glowing silver coin spilling gauzy veils of light onto thin shreds of clouds. Here and there stars pierced the darkness. To the left, a plane left a pale trail across the sky. The air smelled fresh, the night breeze pleasantly cool on my skin.

Quiet.

A shadow dashed across the lit-up driveway, swiped a grocery bag from the back of the Odyssey, and sprinted across the yard to the side of the house before sinking into the night shadows.

Got you, you creepy bastard. If I had blinked, I would've missed it. As it was, I got a vague impression of something simian and large, covered with patchy fur.

The thing on the side of the house ripped the bag apart, tossing the pieces out onto the moonlit lawn. Only its forepaws were visible –ratlike, larger than human hands, with bony hairless fingers armed with sharp black claws. Chunks of a yellow Styrofoam tray followed the bag, and the creature tore into its contents. A crunching noise announced bird bones being crushed. Lovely.

"Baby, did you bring in the groceries?" A woman asked from inside the house.

A muffled male voice answered.

Stay in the house. Stay in the nice safe house.

A woman appeared in the doorway. She was in her early thirties and looked tired, her shoulder-length brown hair messy, her T-shirt rumpled.

The creature dropped its stolen meat.

Stay in the house.

The woman crossed the threshold and headed for the car. The creature melted into the shadows. Either it hid because it was scared or because it was about to strike.

The woman checked the trunk, picked up the lone grocery bag, looked into it and frowned. "Malcolm? Did you take the chicken in?"

No answer.

The monster was nowhere in sight.

Take your bag and go inside.

The woman leaned into the rear passenger door, talking to herself. "I could've sworn... losing my mind."

A flicker of movement on the side of the house, high, about fifteen feet off the ground. I tensed, ready to sprint.

The beast scuttled into the light, crawling along the sheer wall fifteen feet up, like some giant monstrous gecko. It was at least five feet long, maybe five and a half. Spotted black and blue fur grew in patches along its spine; the rest of it was covered with pinkish wrinkled skin. Its skull was almost horselike, if horses could be carnivores. Long jaws, too large for the head, protruded forward, making the wide, flat nose seem ridiculously small. A forest of sharp bloodred fangs sprouted from the jaws, barely hidden by white lips. But the eyes, the eyes were worst of all. Small and sunken deep into the skull, they burned with malevolent intelligence.

The creature gripped the brick wall with oversized digits and dashed across, toward the car, agile like a monkey, too fast for a spear throw. A moment later and it jumped off the wall, clearing the car in one single, powerful lunge, and landed behind the Honda.

Damn it. I hefted my spear and ran.

The woman straightened.

The beast leaned forward, muscles on its four limbs tensing. It looked enormous now. The biggest Great Dane I'd ever seen was four and a half feet long. This beast had a full foot on it.

The creature opened its mouth and growled. A deep, guttural snarl rippled through the night. The hairs on the back of my neck rose. It didn't sound like a dog. It sounded like something dangerous and vicious.

The woman froze.

Don't run, I willed, moving toward them. Whatever you do, don't run. If you run, it will chase and kill you.

The woman took one tiny step toward the door.

The creature slinked behind her and murmured something in a strange language full of whispers and moaning, as if a dozen people lamented and mumbled at once.

"Oh Jesus," the woman whimpered and took another baby step toward the door.

The beast let out a high-pitched cackle. I was almost there.

The woman dashed into the house. The beast chased her. The door slammed shut and the creature rammed it head-on. The door shuddered with a loud thud.

Oh no, you don't. I flipped the spear and thrust. *"Put your weight into it, darling!"* Mom's voice said from my memories. I sank my entire momentum into the spear. The point of the spearhead sliced into the pink, wrinkled flesh, right between the creature's ribs.

The beast howled. White blood bubbled around the wound.

I leaned into the spear and turned, wrenching the impaled creature away from the door and pushing it onto the grass. The monster clawed the lawn, my spear stuck in its ribs like a harpoon. I lunged down, pinning it, and pushed, putting every ounce of strength into the spear, forcing the beast across the grass and into the darkness on the side of the house.

My heart pounded at about a million beats per minute.

The revolting thing screeched, squirming on the end of the spear. If it was human, it would be dead. I should've hit its heart, but it showed no signs of dying. I had to finish it and quickly, before the entire subdivision noticed its screaming and came outside to investigate. I had no clue what its vital organs were or where they were located.

If I couldn't aim for precision, I'd have to go for massive trauma. I freed the spear with a sharp tug. The beast flipped on its feet, impossibly fast, and struck, its long claws like sickles. I shied to the side. Sharp talons raked my left side, searing my ribs with hot pain. I bit on a scream and thrust, aiming for its gut. The beast knocked my spear aside with its shoulder. I whipped the weapon around and drove the butt of the spear into its throat, pinning it to the side of the house. The beast gurgled, scraping at the air with its claws, trying to rend me to pieces. Now, while it was struggling to breathe, or never. I flipped the spear and drove it into the shrunken chest.

Bone crunched. I freed the spear and stabbed it in, again and again, as fast as I could. Stable, powerful thrusts. Another crunch. White blood leaked from the gashes. Sweat drenched my face. The spear felt too heavy.

Another thrust, another, another...

Thick white pus tinted with clumps of pink spilled through the wounds.

The beast sagged. Its horrible clawed hands rose one final time and then fell, limp.

I stabbed it again, just to be sure. My wound burned like someone was sinking red-hot needles into my side. I doubled over. Ow. Ow, ow, ow.

As much as I wanted to dramatically collapse in pain, now was neither the time nor the place. I had to get that cursed thing out of here before somebody saw me.

I surveyed the monster. It was a skinny beast, but still five feet tall. Had to be at least a hundred pounds. Carrying it was out of the question. Not only it was too heavy, but it was bleeding white slime, which could be corrosive or toxic. Dragging it was my best bet.

I concentrated, sending a mental image to the spear. Electric blue veins shot through the weapon. The spearhead curved into a crescent barbed hook. A cross-handle formed toward the foot of the shaft. That would do. I hooked the beast and pulled.

The body slid across the grass. The damn thing was heavy.

A thump followed by a faint creak announced the door of the house swinging open. Great, just what I needed. I spun, weighing my options. I was in a narrow space between two houses. Behind me, a wooden fence guarded the back-yards. The lawn in front of me provided no cover. If I moved into the light to the left, the people would see me. Nowhere to go.

A man swore. "Look at the door."

A woman said, "Oh my God."

Oh my God is right.

A cell phone beeped. "I need to report an attack," the man said. "Something chased my wife..."

I had minutes before the area was crawling with cops. Well, didn't that just take the cake?

The fence belonging to the house on the left had a gate. I reached over it, groping for a lock. My fingers brushed metal. Victory! I flipped the latch. The gate swung open. I hooked the creature, dragged it into the neighboring backyard, and shut the door behind me. So far, so good.

The backyard was empty. Young oaks threw their shadows over the grass and to the right a wooden playhouse crouched in the shadows. Too small and too exposed to offer a good hiding spot. Besides, I couldn't spend my night in the playhouse. I had no idea how long the cops would stay, and dragging the beast home in daylight wasn't an option.

I pulled the creature across the grass to the opposite side of the yard and tried the fence. It was old and weather-beaten.

The distant wail of a siren rolled through the night. Alarm shot through me. I grabbed the old gray wood and pulled. A nail creaked, the wood popped, and a board came free in my hand. I grabbed the next one.

The siren was getting closer.

I yanked the second board off the fence. Here's hoping people in the house were sound sleepers.

The siren screeched, so close.

I pried another board loose, then another. The gap had to be wide enough. I hooked the beast under the ribs and pushed it through the hole. It stuck, wedged. I grabbed its legs and stuffed them through, one at the time, careful not to touch any of the slime. Come on, fit through, you ugly thing.

The siren fell silent. I glanced over my shoulder. Red and blue lights illuminated the night behind me. The cavalry had arrived.

I pushed the last of the beast through the gap and climbed after it. To the right of me, a short palm spread its leaves, flanked by elephant grass. Water splashed.

"Did you hear that?" a woman asked.

I crouched behind the growth. No. No, you didn't hear anything. Don't mind me, I'm not hiding the corpse of a nasty creature behind your flower bed. Nope. Nothing here but cute, fluffy bunnies scampering adorably into the night...

"Hear what?" a man asked.

"The sirens, Kevin."

"No."

Kevin was my kind of people.

"Kevin..."

Water splashed. "I've got the only siren I care about right here."

Hello there, Mr. Smooth.

The woman giggled.

I leaned forward and peeked out from behind the greenery. A pool spread in front of me. Solar lights floated on the water, dappling the bottom with red and yellow circles. At the far end a man and woman in their forties sat on a step, half-submerged.

"Come on," Kevin murmured. "Kids are asleep, the water is warm, the moon is out... I have the wine. We should drink the wine and then..."

"Would you like to fool around?" the woman asked.

"I wouldn't be opposed, no."

She put her arms around his neck. "Getting romantic in your old age?"

The shrubs at the edge of the pool were too short. I could possibly sneak by if I moved fast while they were distracted. If I tried to drag the body, they'd definitely see me.

I looked at the house. Directly in front of me, on the second floor, the curtains were open. An iPod charging station sat on the windowsill next to a stuffed teddy bear. Kid room.

More giggling.

I snuck along the shrubs, sprinted to the side of the house, and held my breath.

"Mmm, taking charge of the situation...," the woman purred.

"You love it, baby."

I almost felt bad, but I had no choice. I put my hand against the house. I was much weaker outside the inn, but I could still manage a basic push.

The inner workings of the house spread before me, the structural beams, the long stretches of pipe, and the spider work of wiring. I singled out the right wire and sent a gentle nudge.

The iPod station blared, spilling Nicki Minaj into the night.

The pool fell silent.

Something crashed above me. The music died.

"Mom?" a young female voice said. "Is that you?"

"Yes," the woman answered. "Go back to sleep."

"Is that Dad? Are the two of you doing it in the pool? Ew!"

Kevin growled.

Another window slid open and a boy's voice called out. "What's going on?"

"Mom and Dad are doing it in the pool."

"Ugh."

"Nobody is doing anything!" Kevin barked. "Go back to bed!"

"You know you can get diseases from doing that, right? The pool water isn't sanitary…"

"It definitely won't be sanitary after they're done with it," the boy quipped.

"Back to bed! Now!"

The windows closed.

Kevin groaned. "How long until they finish high school and go off to college?"

"Three years."

"I don't think I can hold out that long."

"Why don't we grab our wine and take it inside?" the woman said. "We can go to our giant comfortable bedroom, lock the door, and drink wine. In bed."

"That's a great idea."

A couple of minutes later, the door thudded closed. I waited a little while longer to be on the safe side and resumed my dragging. If my arms didn't fall off, the cops didn't bust me, and the amorous suburb residents stayed in their houses, I might even make it home in half an hour or so.

An hour later I trudged to the side gate of my wooden fence. It opened in anticipation and I stepped through onto the inn grounds. Power coursed through me. The spear-hook flowed back into the broom.

The dog door in the northern entrance swung open and Beast dashed out. She licked my feet, growled at the dead creature, and ran around me in a circle.

"Everything quiet while I was gone?"

The Beast dived at my feet again and licked my shoe.

"Take him to the basement," I said.

The lawn under the body opened and the corpse fell through. The dirt and grass closed behind it and smoothed themselves out.

I went inside. The floorboards of the lobby parted at my approach, folding back on themselves and dropping down to form a stairway that led under the house. The stairs ran into the steel door. I descended and touched the metal. Magic licked my palm. A complex pattern of dark blue hairline cracks formed on the door and it slid aside. I walked in.

The lamp that was suspended in the middle of the room ignited, drenching the steel table below it in a white glow. The dead creature was lying on it and looked just as revolting as I remembered.

To the left and right, mood lamps came on in their wall sconces, their yellow light soothing and comfortable, in sharp contrast to the sterility of the lab lamp. Shelves lined the far wall, filled to the brink with books, while glass cabinets containing jars and containers in every size and shape occupied the other two walls. To the right, a concrete-and-tile decontamination shower stood waiting its chance to shine in the event of an emergency.

"Thank you." I touched the table. "Secure, please."

Metal strips curled from the table's corners, locking the creature's four limbs in place. I didn't think it would come back to life, but you never know. Stranger things have happened. I put on a pair of scrubs, safety goggles and slipped on a pair of gloves.

The beast lay on its back, its wrinkled, hairless belly exposed. Ugly critter.

Time for the *Creature Guide*. I pulled a thick book from
the shelf and waved my fingers above it. The book flipped
through the pages, reacting to my magic. Looking things
up manually was a centuries-old tradition, as ancient as the
inns themselves. The advent of computers hadn't changed
anything. In the event of a Law Enforcement Breach, a
computer would the first thing the LEOs –law enforcement officers –would confiscate. I had a laptop upstairs in
plain view, partially for that exact purpose. They were welcome to my Twitter account and my gallery of cute fluffy
animals dressed in hilarious Halloween costumes. Nobody
thought to check the dead-tree books anymore, and even
if they did, they would likely mistake the *Guide* for a novelty
volume.

This copy of the *Creature Guide* was old. The inn itself was
late nineteenth century, but the *Creature Guide* had a mottled
leather binding with some gold tooling on the cover, which
put it at least two centuries earlier. The prior owner of the
inn must've inherited it from another innkeeper. As soon as
I gained access to some funds, I'd have to get a more recent
version.

The book was indexed by several criteria. I decided on
Breathing. It was the most obvious choice and would let me
knock a fair number of species off my list. The page offered
me a long list of codes. I took a pair of forceps from the tray
and pulled the beast's nose open. Nothing obstructed the
four nasal passages. The air didn't seem to have had any
adverse or toxic effects on it. I noted the codes for Nitrogen,
Oxygen, Argon, CO_2 and Neon, and continued.

Symmetry: bilateral. If you drew a line along the beast's
body from nose to the tail, the left side would be the mirror
image of the right. Habitat: tentatively terrestrial. It didn't
have any gills, fins, feathers, or digging claws. Blood: white.

A page of chemical tests presented itself, and I took a few samples and set to work.

Half an hour later I had the code range and pulled another thick volume from the shelf. "M4K6G-UR174-8LAN3-9800L-E86VA." Say that three times fast.

The pages rustled. My analysis gave me roughly one hundred and thirty-two possibilities. Luckily for me, the descriptions came with pictures. Let's see... No, no, ew, no, how did this thing even move, no... I kept turning the pages, and when a familiar revolting image appeared, I almost blew right by it.

Ma'avi Kerras. The Ma'avi Stalker family. *Predatory, deadly, hunts by sight and scent, travels in packs.* Packs. Great. The intelligence scale indicated the stalkers ranked between forty six and fifty eight, about as smart as the average baboon, which made them quite intelligent for the animal kingdom and very dangerous. Not intelligent enough to travel to the inn by themselves, however. Someone had brought this lovely creature here, to Red Deer, and let it loose on an unsuspecting populace. Had it been dumped here and left to wreak havoc? Why? By whom? Where were its masters?

I read the article again. It was more like a stub, a brief summary, than an in-depth description. I needed more data. I sighed. It's one thing to know your archives are woefully inadequate, but it's a completely different ball game when your nose is rubbed in it.

The stalker was dead. Even if I had somehow managed to take it alive, it didn't have the brainpower to spill the proverbial beans. Cutting it into small pieces would be satisfying –my ribs still hurt –but futile.

I pulled off my gloves. If only Mom and Dad were still here...

The heartache mugged me. I squeezed my eyes tight against the hurt and wished with everything I had that they would walk through the door. My magic rolled from me in a powerful wave.

The inn creaked in alarm.

Nice going. I was scaring the house.

I opened my eyes. They weren't there. Of course they weren't.

"It's all right." I petted the wall. "It's just a human thing. I miss them, that's all."

Further research would have to wait till morning when my head was clearer. I told the house to refrigerate my evidence and went upstairs to take a shower, treat my wounds, and swallow a couple of painkillers.

CHAPTER THREE

Beast raised her head and growled. I opened my eyes. I was sitting in a soft, oversized chair, trying to cure my headache with a cup of coffee. Dealing with intruders was the next to last thing on my want-to-do list this morning, the last thing being anything that involved werewolves.

My wounds had turned out to be shallow. The claws had barely grazed my ribs –it still hurt like there was no tomorrow –and once properly treated, most of it was on the mend. Unfortunately, dawn brought me the gift of a splitting headache, and a thousand milligrams of painkiller wasn't even making a dent in it. I finally gave up on sleeping, crawled downstairs, made coffee, and settled down into the chair in the front seating area to drink my poison in peace.

My parents looked at me from the photograph on the wall. *Yes, I went off the inn grounds and involved myself in some terrible mess. You would have too, in my position.*

Beast barked, her gaze fixed on the screen door.

No peace for the wicked.

The magic splashed around me. Incoming. It could be a guest, although most guests would be more polite.

I leaned over to glance outside through the screen door. Sean Evans was marching across my yard, emitting menace. His face was grim and his eyes betrayed steely determination. All those hard muscles finally revealed their true purpose –they were propelling his big body toward me at an alarming speed and their strength guaranteed he'd mow down whatever was in his way. If I shut the door, he'd go right through it. That's how the medieval knights must've looked when they assaulted a castle.

I looked at Beast. "Raise the drawbridge."

The tiny dog gazed at me, puzzled.

"You're a terrible gatekeeper."

Sean pounded on the screen door's frame. "I know you're in there."

"Should we let him in?" I asked Beast.

"I can hear you," he snarled.

So he could. I sighed. "Okay. Come in. It's unlocked."

He yanked the door open and strode into the house. "Where is it?"

"Good morning to you too, sunshine."

"I said where is it?"

"Not so loud. I have a headache."

He leaned over, planting his hands on the arms of my chair. His amber eyes were all but glowing. Sean Evans was officially pissed off. *Serves you right, furball.*

"What did you do with it?"

"I have no idea what you're talking about." I drank my coffee.

"You went out and killed it last night and then you dragged it back here."

I gave him my best innocent look. "Sir, I think you might be crazy."

"You left a scent trail a mile long and I tracked it to this house. You took my kill and got hurt doing it."

"What makes you think that?"

"I smelled your blood. What the hell possessed you to go out there? I said I was handling it."

Oh, that was rich. "Handling what? I asked you to take care of it. You blew me off and decided to limit your involvement to poisoning my apples."

"Poisoning? Really?" He actually sputtered.

I'd wanted him to handle it because I hadn't wanted to break my neutrality and he was uniquely suited to killing things. But now that ship had sailed, and given his attitude, I was better off without his so-called help. I leaned forward so we were eye to eye. "It's being handled. Your involvement isn't necessary. You're free to continue on your serial urination spree."

"I don't think so."

"Sean! Go. Away."

He locked his jaw. "I don't know what the hell is going on here, but I'm not leaving until I get it sorted out."

Of all the rude, arrogant morons... "Is that so?"

"Yes. You will show that thing to me and from now on, *I* will deal with them."

I opened my eyes really wide and fluttered my eyelashes at him. "I'm sorry, I must've missed your coronation ceremony. Silly me."

"Dina!"

Ha! He remembered my name. I waved my fingers in the direction of the door. "Shoo. Leave, and don't slam the door on your way out."

He planted himself, arms crossed, muscles bulging. "Make me."

He didn't deserve a warning, but I gave him one anyway. "I've had about enough. I'm serious, Sean. Leave or there will be consequences."

"Give me your best shot."

Fine. "Your welcome is withdrawn."

Magic smashed into Sean. He went airborne. The side door swung open just in time and he flew through it and into the orchard. The orchard was a safer bet. The bulk of the house shielded it from the passersby and traffic, which would hopefully let us avoid pain-in-the-butt questions.

I heard a solid thud, then got up, and looked out through the open door. Beast joined me.

Sean lay unmoving on the grass. Ouches.

I glanced at Beast. "I did warn him."

Sean raised his head, shook it, and rolled to his feet. His face gained that feral, predatory look.

"Uh-oh. We better brace ourselves." I sipped from my coffee cup.

Sean took a running start and charged through the door. It started to close, and I flicked my fingers, telling the inn to keep it open. The door would cost money to replace. Sean thrust through the doorway, got a foot and a half inside, and the magic punched him again, hurtling him backward. Sean flew, rolling on the grass as he fell.

He shouldn't have made it that far in. He shouldn't have been able to enter, period. True, the inn had stood abandoned for a long while and wasn't as strong as most yet, but it should've kept him out.

Sean jumped to his feet. His eyes had gone completely savage. He gathered himself into a tight ball and sprinted to the door with inhuman speed. I felt the inn block him. He smashed into the invisible barrier and tore through it, managing to get two steps inside.

The magic hit him, throwing him backward. He caught the doorframe with his hands and hung on.

Whoa.

Sean growled like an animal. It was a bone-chilling sound that no human being had a right to make.

I picked up my broom. The inn would need some help. "You know what the definition of insanity is, Beast?"

Sean strained. The muscles on his arms and body bulged, taut like ropes under his skin. Slowly he gained an inch. Another inch. Wow. He was remarkably strong.

"According to Einstein, it's doing the same thing over and over and expecting a different result." I brought the butt of the broom down on the floor. "*Out.*"

My magic *boomed* through the inn like the toll of a huge bell. It had no sound, but I heard it all the same. Sean flew out of the house like a fleck of dust caught in the current of a fan and smashed into an apple tree forty feet away. I heard the crunch all the way from where I stood.

"Karma," I said, petting the doorframe.

The house creaked.

"You did well," I murmured to it. "He's just freakishly powerful."

Unbelievably powerful. I've handled werewolves before. They were psychotic and homicidal, but none could've done what he did.

Sean wasn't moving. Maybe the impact had broken something. Not that he wouldn't heal –he would, and at an accelerated rate –but still, snapping his spine hadn't been my intention.

Beast brushed against my ankle.

"Should we go investigate?"

The magic tugged on me. I leaned back to glance through the front door. A black-and-white was parked by my driveway and a man in a tan uniform marched up said driveway to my house. I was about to get a visit from Red Deer PD. I spun back around.

The grass under the apple tree was empty. Sean Evans had vanished.

"Can I offer you some tea, Officer?"

Officer Hector Marais peered at me. Solid and fit, clean-shaven, his dark hair cut short, he embodied the very essence of his profession. If you saw him dressed in jeans and a hoodie, walking toward you at dusk, you wouldn't cross the street, because you would know he was a cop. He radiated that air of wary authority, and as he crossed the threshold into the inn, he surveyed me and then the interior of the inn as if he was looking for weapons.

"No, thank you, Ms. Demille. There was a disturbance in your subdivision last night, around one in the morning. A woman was attacked. Have you noticed anything unusual?"

"Oh my goodness. Who was it? Is she okay? What happened?" People who had prior awareness of the incident didn't ask questions.

Officer Marais studied me. "The victim is fine. We're classifying it as a wild animal attack. Did you notice anything unusual last night? Noises, perhaps an uncommonly large animal?"

"No. Should I be locking my door?"

"You should always lock your door. Are you aware of anyone who keeps exotic pets?"

"Robyn Kay has a pet lizard," I told him. "I think it's an iguana."

Officer Marais pulled out a notepad and made a notation on it. "Address?"

"She lives at Igraine Court. I don't recall the house number. It's a brick house with a large prickly pear cactus in front."

"What about anyone having a mountain lion or a bear?"

I shook my head. "I've never heard of anyone having a bear or a mountain lion. We would know. People in this neighborhood don't have many secrets."

"You would be surprised," he said.

You don't know the half of it.

"Are you aware that several dogs in your neighborhood have been killed recently?"

"Oh, yes. It's horrible."

"We have a reason to believe someone in this area is keeping a large predatory animal as a pet." He nodded at Beast. "I advise you to make sure your dog is always on a leash and is supervised when it's allowed outside."

"She."

Officer Marais blinked.

"She's a girl," I told him.

Beast barked once to underscore the point.

Officer Marais pulled out a business card, plain white with blue print on it. "If you become aware of someone keeping an exotic pet or see it, please give me a call. Do not approach the animal."

"Of course."

"Have you had any more trouble with teenagers?"

He remembered. Three years ago, shortly after I first moved into the inn, Caldenia had arrived with a small herd of bounty hunters at her heels. A couple of them had proved to be dumb enough to try to snipe her. I'd dealt with them almost instantly, but not before Mr. Ramirez down the street reported shots fired to the police. Officer Marais had been in one of the four responding police cars.

Since the inn had hid the damage and it was just after New Year's, I claimed some kids had shot off leftover fireworks. Unfortunately, Mr. Ramirez was a retired Marine, and he'd been adamant that he heard rifle shots. In the absence of evidence, the cops' had no choice but to leave, but it was pretty clear Officer Marais hadn't bought my story.

"No trouble at all," I said.

Officer Marais gave me one last look-over. "Thank you for your cooperation, ma'am. Please let me know if you become aware of anything pertaining to this case. Good-bye."

"Good-bye."

I watched him walk to his car. Most people discounted intuition as a nonexistent superstition. I knew better. Whenever I'd get too bratty with my powers, Dad used to remind me that every human had magic. The difference between them and me was awareness and practice. Most people simply didn't realize they could do things that bent their reality. It was kind of like growing up in a land with no deep rivers or lakes. If you never tried, how would you know if you could swim?

But even without practice, the magic found a way to make itself known. Intuition was such a manifestation. Officer Marais's intuition was telling him loud and clear that there was something wrong with me. He couldn't put his finger on it, but his tenacity wouldn't let him just move on. Even though the incident happened several streets away, he decided to visit me just in case. Now that he had a reason to come back and keep checking on the neighborhood, I'd have to watch my step.

Speaking of intuition... Something about my conversation with Sean was bugging me. I puzzled over it and realized what it was. He'd said, "From now on, I'll deal with them." Them. As in more than one. The *Creature Guide* said that stalkers traveled in packs, but Sean had no way of knowing that. If he had access to a resource that could identify stalkers, it could also identify me, and he would've adjusted his attitude instead of storming my castle.

He must've smelled different scents. Maybe throwing him out wasn't such a hot idea. No, no, it was. There were limits. No matter how powerful he was, I couldn't let him run hog wild over the inn and me.

"Them" meant the incidents would keep happening. Whoever was behind this would soon realize I had taken out one of the pack. He or she could retaliate, and I had no idea what form that retaliation would take. Save for an abbreviated entry in the *Creature Guide*, my search on stalkers hadn't turned up anything useful. They were a rare species, not too numerous and not well-known.

I could look through the rest of my resources. I had access to some other books, but I doubted I'd find anything useful. I'd have to look for any casual mention of the stalkers in association with other species, and none of the other volumes were indexed or searchable. They were mostly anecdotes recorded by various innkeepers.

When I was eight, my parents had taken me, my brother, and my sister to California on vacation. We'd visited many cool places, including Glass Beach near the town of Fort Bragg. The residents of the area used to toss garbage into the ocean, a lot of which consisted of glass, and over the years, the waves had smoothed the sharp shards into beautiful glass pebbles and deposited thousands of them back onto the beach. In the grand scheme of things, looking for the stalkers was like going to Glass Beach near Fort Bragg and trying to find a particular piece of glass among thousands of others. It would take a long time, and my time was in short supply.

I missed my sister. Unlike my brother, who occasionally dropped by would he could tear himself away from the great beyond, she never visited. She fell in love, married, and moved with her husband to his planet. I had no idea what her new life was like, I hoped it was nice.

I needed a shortcut. I needed someone with more experience and practical knowledge.

I walked over to the photograph of my parents and pressed my thumb to a wood whorl in the frame. A small notation appeared in the top corner above my mother's head.

Brian Rodriguez, 8200 Cielo Vista, Dallas.
I let go of the frame and the words faded. Brian Rodriguez was an innkeeper. He didn't know me and I didn't know him, but my father had mentioned him before. Mr. Rodriguez operated one of the oldest inns in Texas, which had stood there when the Viceroyalty of New Spain was still a real power. Unlike Gertrude Hunt, that inn had remained continuously occupied with the knowledge and expertise passed from one innkeeper to the next. If anyone knew about stalkers, it would be Mr. Rodriguez.

Dallas was over four hours away by car. If I left now, I could theoretically be back here before midnight. Unless I broke down on the highway. I doubted anything would occur during the day, but once darkness fell, without me the inn would be fair game. If stalkers, their allies, or Sean, decided to retaliate, tonight would present them with an excellent opportunity.

I sat down and gulped my tea. I'd never met Mr. Rodriguez. My father had spoken of him in flattering terms, and I'd been there when my mother had written his name and address on the portrait. I was told he was knowledgeable and I could ask him for advice. However, he wasn't a friend. When my parents vanished, I had written to him and received no reply.

Trying to phone him would be useless –no innkeeper would respond to a phone inquiry. The innkeepers were neutral entities and we operated covertly and independently of each other, separated by distance. The safety of our guests was our highest priority. We relied on first impressions and handshakes and did business face-to-face only.

If I made the trip to Dallas, there was no guarantee Mr. Rodriguez would even answer my questions.

What to do?

Sitting here waiting for the stalkers to make the first move was pointless. I had no idea what their avenue of attack would be. I didn't even have a clear idea what they were capable off. Was there some intelligence behind them pulling their strings or were they dumped here just to wreak havoc?

Leaving the inn was a risk, but it was a risk I had to take. I'd chosen to become involved –which might have been a mistake on my part, but now it was too late to second-guess it –and I needed to take steps to ensure the security of the inn. Forewarned is forearmed.

Besides, I'd overhauled the inn's security in the past three years. We'd run drills and tested different scenarios. The inn wasn't impregnable with me away, but breaking into it was impossible without making a lot of noise. I had a feeling noise was the last thing anyone wanted.

If I was going to go, I had to go now. At the moment Caldenia was my only guest, and she would stay safely in her quarters. But if another guest suddenly made an appearance, my trip would be canceled.

I got up and went upstairs to the northern balcony. Caldenia sat in her favorite chair, gazing at the street. She saw me and motioned with her long fingers. "Look. I find this extremely curious."

I sat next to her. Below us, a pair of cops was trying to calm two bloodhounds. The big goofy dogs shifted back and forth on their leashes. Officer Marais and another policeman looked on.

Finally one of the K9 officers got his dog under control and said something. The bloodhound obediently put its nose to the asphalt, took three steps forward, and backed away, whining, tail between its legs.

"Are they sensing the creature you brought in last night?"

"They are sensing Sean Evans."

Last night, as I was forced to hide in a bush with my grisly prize, I'd realized the creature's white blood was evaporating in the open air within about five minutes. The only way anyone would be able to track me would be by drag marks or scent. So I'd taken a risk and moved onto the road, dragging my corpse in plain view, ready to bolt or hide at the slightest noise. Eventually I'd made it to Uther Street, which connected to Igraine Road. I'd been about to turn onto Igraine when I saw Sean, a huge shaggy shadow, pure black, running on all fours. He'd dashed down Camelot and I'd sagged against the nearest fence to have a moment, afraid my heart might jump out of my chest because it was beating so fast.

The second bloodhound danced in place and howled, a hysterical, frightened wail.

"Last night he was reinforcing his signature," I said. "My guess is that he's ambitious as to what he considers his territory, so he must've gone quite far to mark his boundaries. Then when police showed up, curiosity got the better of him, and Sean turned to covert mode so he could close the distance fast, sneak up close, and see what was happening. His pheromone trail is all over the street."

The werewolves had three basic modes: their human form, which has the highest dexterity, they called the OPS form —operations; their wetwork form, a humanoid, wolflike monster for close and personal combat; and the OM, on-the-move, a covert form for rapidly and quietly covering great distances. When they shifted from one shape to another, the chemical cocktail in their bodies caused a release of pheromones that freaked out anything on four legs. Mrs. Zhu, an older werewolf who used to frequent my parents' inn, had told me the pheromone release was a deliberate signal, programmed into them but not under their direct control. When on a mission, it helped to know that other members of your group had changed shape without visual signs or sounds to give you away.

The neighborhood dogs had no problem with Sean the human. Sean the "wolf," however, made them hysterical. I was told that the pheromone emissions stopped within fifteen minutes or so of the transformation, they had left a lasting scent signature. Sean had freshly turned. I gambled that his scent would be strong and my gamble proved right. His pheromones freaked the bloodhounds out so much, they refused to follow his trail and since my trail lay in the same direction, they refused to follow it as well. With no blood and no scent trail, nobody had any reason to connect the inn and me with claw marks on the door of a house several streets away.

As if on cue, Officer Marais turned and looked directly at us.

"He suspects something," Caldenia said.

"He has no proof."

"If he ever becomes an issue, I could eat him. He looks delicious."

"Thank you, but that won't be necessary." And that wasn't creepy. Not at all.

Caldenia smiled. "You will be surprised how difficult it is to get rid of a human body. I'd say he is perhaps a hundred and seventy pounds? That's a lot of flesh to manage. We could freeze it. He'd feed me for at least three months."

He also was happily married with two small daughters. I had Googled him after our first encounter and found his wife's blog. She worked as a therapist and liked to knit.

CLEAN SWEEP

"I need to leave," I said. "I should be back today before midnight. Please stay inside."

"I will. I have a brand new Eloisa James book to keep me company."

Ten minutes later, my backpack was packed. I went back to the lobby.

The house creaked around me.

"I'll be back tonight." I petted the wall. "Don't worry. Security Protocol AWAY in sixty seconds."

I petted Beast, grabbed my keys, and stepped outside. The Shih Tzu whined quietly.

"Guard the house. She may need help. I'll be back soon."

I pulled the car out of the garage and waited for a few moments on the street, counting backward. Five, four, three, two… One.

The house clanged. From outside nothing had changed, but I knew that inside shutters slid closed behind the glass and curtains. The two doors visible from the street locked and barred themselves, the two less obvious doors had melted completely into the walls. The inn became a fortress that would defend itself and record everything that transpired while I was gone.

Drive at speed limit, get to Dallas, visit, get back. Do not linger. I started down the street. The sooner I got there, the sooner I could get back.

47

CHAPTER FOUR

I-45 stretched before me, a flat ribbon of asphalt bordered on both sides by short trees, mesquite, ash, and oak. The car sped forward, chomping down the miles. I always liked driving. My mother had too.

My father had been born in a time when a galloping horse was the top speed a man could attain. The moment he'd get into a car, he'd begin what my mother used to affectionately call the Gerard Show. At the start of the drive he'd sit perfectly still in the passenger seat, gripping the door with white-knuckled strength, his face a pale, rigid mask of grim determination, his eyes wide open. This lasted until we encountered traffic, at which point he would start pointing out cars and road hazards in this quiet emergency voice. He would close his eyes and brace himself when we switched lanes. If we had to come to a stop before a red light and another vehicle had gotten there before us, he would throw his hands in front of his face or sometimes in front of Mom's body, trying to shield her, when we came to a stop. One time we were on the road and a giant semi veered a little too close. He'd screamed, "Jesu, Helen, turn the horses!" and then spent the rest of the day being embarrassed about it.

I'd once had a teacher with a severe airplane anxiety. She'd told me that every time she stepped on a plane, she'd done so with a full expectation that she was going to die. She had made a folder with a skull and crossbones on it, which contained her will and life insurance policy and would make sure to leave it in plain view so her family wouldn't have to "scramble for information" in case of her death. My father, who was the bravest man I had ever known, had a similar mindset: every time he entered a vehicle, he did it with the expectation that he –or Mom and me, which was infinitely worse for him –wouldn't survive the trip. Every car ride was a near-death experience.

Despite all this, Mom did somehow teach him to drive. Very occasionally, when he absolutely had to, he would drive the car down a quiet street for a mile and a half to the grocery store and gas station. We weren't allowed to go with him because he refused to be responsible for our deaths. He never let it get faster than thirty-five miles per hour. When he returned, armed with groceries, he would park the vehicle in the driveway, get out, and lay on the grass, looking at the sky for about ten minutes. Sometimes I would come and lay with him. We'd look at the sky and the trees rustling above us and be happy we were alive.

I missed them both so badly. I would find them. Someone somewhere had to know something about them. One day that someone would walk into my inn, see the portrait of my parents on the wall, and I would see that knowledge on his or her face. And then I would find my parents.

My GPS came on and Darth Vader prompted me to take the next exit. Ten minutes later, after bearing left "to the dark side," I parked before a large house. It sat recessed from the street, behind tall, slender palms and acacias, and I could barely make out the peach stucco walls under terra-cotta tile roof. A winding stone path led across the grass toward the house.

I crossed the street and stopped before the walkway. Ghostly bugs skittered across my skin. The small hairs on my arms rose. I was on the edge of another inn's grounds. I took a step forward. The magic rolled over me. I braced myself and stood still, waiting. If the innkeeper didn't want me to enter, he would let me know. My father was well regarded because before he'd become an innkeeper, he'd been a guest, and he had chosen to risk his life to help the owner of an inn. It had cost him centuries of incarceration and solitude. But he had his detractors as well. If I was lucky, Mr. Rodriguez wasn't one the latter.

Silence stretched. Birds chirped in the trees above me. A minute chugged by. Another. Long enough. Since nobody came to throw me out, I must be welcome.

I started down the path. The air smelled fresh and clean, with a hint of moisture. The path turned and I saw the source of the humidity: a shallow pond bending in natural curves in the center of a beautifully tiled courtyard. Orange-and-white koi moved ponderously through a foot of green water. Around the pond, plants thrived in bordered flower beds: bright red and yellow canna flowers with big leaves, small purple and scarlet clusters of verbena, and dandelion-gold stars of yellow bush daisy. Short palms and artfully pruned mesquite provided shade for aged wooden benches with wrought-iron frames. Beyond the courtyard curved the house, a two-story-high semicircle of arcades, shady balconies with ornate columns, arches, and wooden doorways.

Various traces of magic signatures slid past me, footprints of power left by dozens of guests. This was a thriving inn, frequented by many creatures of different talents. My parents' inn used to feel this way too: strong and vibrant. Alive. If this inn was a floodlight, Gertrude Hunt would be a flame in a lone lantern by comparison. That's okay, I promised myself. One day...

A man crouched by one of the flower beds, carefully digging at the soil with a hand rake. He looked to be in his late fifties, with silver in his dark hair and naturally bronze skin, weathered by time and the elements into deep wrinkles. A short, carefully trimmed beard hugged his jaw. A young woman stood next to him in a conservative blue dress and silvery pumps, her dark hair curled into a stylish updo. She was a couple of years older than me, but the look on her face was unmistakable. It was the look that any child past twelve would recognize and could perfectly duplicate. It said "I'm being chewed out by my parent. Again. Can you believe this?"

"...If I wanted to handle it myself, Isabella, I wouldn't have requested your help."

Oh no, not the patient-dad voice.

"The entire point of delegating a task is so one doesn't have to perform it himself."

Isabella sighed. "Yes, Father. You have a visitor."

"I'm perfectly aware of her, thank you." The man fixed me with sharp dark eyes. "May I help you?"

Coming here was probably a mistake. "My father once told me that I could ask a man here for advice."

"What was his name?"

"Brian Rodriguez."

The man nodded patiently. "I know what my name is. What was *your father's* name?"

"Gerard Demille."

The man studied me. "Gerard Demille? You're Gerard and Helen's daughter?"

I nodded.

He got up. "Thank you, Issy, that will be all."

Isabella sighed again. "Does this mean you're done lecturing me?"

"Yes. To answer your question, tell the ifrit that if they want the use of the formal dining room, we'll need something from their khan stating they will handle the expenses. That will quiet them right up." He pointed at the bench. "Please sit."

Isabella turned and went toward the house, shaking her head. I sat on the bench next to him.

"Dina Demille," Brian Rodriquez said. He had a deep, slightly raspy voice. "When I heard that you'd moved in to Gertrude Hunt, I thought you would come to visit me sooner."

"I wasn't sure I would be welcome."

"My dear, your father put his own life in jeopardy for the sake of an innkeeper's wife and children. You're very young, so you probably don't have enough experience to realize how rarely a guest risks himself for our sake. Gerard is a very brave man."

"He would say he is very foolish."

"He would. For all of his bluster and pretending to be a scoundrel, he was always a modest man. All innkeepers owe him a debt of gratitude, and your mother selflessly saved him from the eternity of imprisonment. As their daughter, you are always welcome at this inn. What made you doubt that?"

"You didn't answer my letter."

"What letter?"

"I sent you a letter after the incident. It was some years ago."

Mr. Rodriguez shook his head. "I never received it. What did you write?" He seemed completely genuine.

"I asked if you knew anything about their disappearance." A tiny, fragile hope fluttered its wings in my chest.

Mr. Rodriguez leaned forward. "In a word, no. People can and do disappear from time to time, but for an entire inn to simply vanish is unheard of. Your parents were well thought of. When the incident occurred, I checked into it and many others did, too. But our collective wisdom failed. We know nothing."

The hope died. I did my best to hide my disappointment.

"You must miss them," he said.

"I do." Every single day.

"I'm sorry."

"Thank you."

Mr. Rodriguez offered me a small smile. "So, what may I do for you, daughter of Gerard and Helen?"

I took out a photograph of the stalker and passed it to him.

Mr. Rodriguez stared at the photograph. Alarm flared in his eyes.

"A Ma'avi stalker. Nasty creatures, vindictive and cruel. Is the inn threatened?"

"Yes." Technically, it was threatened now that I had gotten myself involved. "The stalker began killing dogs, then escalated. I believe there is more than one of them. How did they get here?"

"The same as everyone else." Mr. Rodriguez studied the photograph. "The question is why and who brought them in. You've had no unusual guests?"

"Only Caldenia."

"Ahh, yes. Not many people would've taken her in. I imagine she pays well, but the trouble she brings can't possibly be worth the fee."

"It's wasn't the money," I told him. "Although it was welcome. The inn needed a guest."

Brian smiled. "Ahh. Your parents would be proud. People of your age don't always understand that simple truth: the inns require guests to flourish."

My parents had never turned away a guest, no matter how difficult they were to accommodate. It was simply the way they did things. I saw no reason to veer from that course. Mr. Rodriguez tapped the photograph. "Years ago, when I was much younger, my parents sent me to the West Coast to take care of some private business. I stayed at the Blue Falls, a very specialized inn. It catered to high-risk guests. One of them was something called a dahaka. He was in the lobby when I came in and I had to wait for about five minutes until he finished his business. It was thirty years ago, and I remember it like it was yesterday. He wore armor, carried high-technology rifles, and had two stalkers sitting by his feet. Being in his presence was like being trapped in a cage with a vicious, hungry animal. I felt the menace. He emitted it like fire emits heat. His stalkers drooled at me. I saw the hunger in their eyes. To them I was prey. Food."

He shivered and shook his head. "The dahaka looked at me in passing as he went to his room. It felt like somebody dumped a bucket of ice water over my head. Every hair on my body stood up." He rubbed his forearm. "I was a young kid then, twenty. I had all these powers and I thought I was immortal. That was the moment when I realized I could die."

This didn't sound good. Not at all. "And he had stalkers with him?"

Mr. Rodriguez nodded. "Dahaka are a reclusive and very violent race. They pride themselves on their ability to kill, and they often employ other creatures the way our hunters employ dogs. Stalkers are some of their favorites."

I thought out loud. "But why would a dahaka be in Red Deer, Texas? There's nothing there. And if one of them was there, why wouldn't he come to the inn?"

"I don't know. But I can tell you there's one way to find out if you have a dahaka. They implant transmitters into their animals. If you have one, that stalker corpse has a transmitter somewhere in its flesh."

So I was facing a very violent creature armed with advanced weaponry and a pack of murderous beasts. How in the world would I even deal with it?

"I wish I could help," Mr. Rodriguez said.

"Thank you." We both knew he couldn't. He had his inn and I had mine. "I just wish the inn was stronger, that's all."

"Would you mind a bit of unsolicited advice?"

"I'll take all the advice I can get."

He turned and nodded at the inn. "Casa Feliz is a very busy place. We serve Dallas and Fort Worth and a good deal of Oklahoma. We have a reputable standing as a good place to stay for most guests. In essence, we are the Holiday Inn of our world."

Yes, his inn was doing well and mine wasn't. I was painfully aware of that fact. "I'm afraid I don't follow."

"When Gertrude Hunt was built all those years ago, it stood on a road crossing. But now the roads have moved on, the inn stood abandoned, and I would guess that even with proximity to Austin and Houston, you still don't get many visitors. My point is that there are different kinds of inns. Some inns are like Casa Feliz and cater to a wide variety of patrons. Some cater only to few, select customers. The guests with special needs. Don't fight your remote location –turn it to your advantage. If you succeed in that, you'll build a quiet reputation that will speak volumes. Your exclusivity could be an asset, the way it was for Blue Falls."

"Thank you." It was sound advice. I just had no idea how to follow it. "May I trouble you for an introduction to the Blue Falls innkeeper? Perhaps I could call him and ask him for more information about dahakas?"

Mr. Rodriguez shook his head. "I'm sorry, but Blue Falls was destroyed seventeen years ago. One of the guests went on a rampage and murdered the innkeeper and her family. A terrible tragedy."

Umm. So I could be just like that other innkeeper who'd died in a horrible way.

I rose off the bench. "Thank you so much for all your help. I must be going."

"You've driven a long way. Would you like some lunch?"

"No, thank you. I want to get back as soon as possible."

Mr. Rodriguez nodded. "I understand. If there is anything else I can do, don't hesitate to call. I'll help in any way I can."

I started down the path. Oh, shoot, Sean. "Mr. Rodriguez?"

"Yes?"

"Do you know why a particular werewolf would be much stronger than others?"

Mr. Rodriguez smiled and said in the patient voice he'd used with Isabella, "Have you consulted your *Creature Guide*?"

"I have. It doesn't mention anything relevant."

"Did you inherit it with the inn?"

"Yes. All my books and possessions disappeared with my parents."

Mr. Rodriguez nodded. "It's probably out of date. Before the werewolves blew themselves up, they bred a second generation of combat operatives to hold the gates against the Sun Horde while the population evacuated. They're just like the usual werewolves, except more: stronger, faster, harder to kill, more aggressive, more everything. They aren't too stable, but nobody worried about that at the time since they weren't expected to live. The funny thing is, their makers bred them to survive against overwhelming odds, holding the gates against superior firepower often by pure will, and then were extremely surprised when their creations refused to give up and die at the end. Most of the second generation did perish in the final blast, but several units made it through the gates. They are rare and other werewolves stay away from them. Some would say that they are ostracized or even shunned, others argue that we simply give them the distance and respect that their sacrifice and heroic combat performance demanded. It all depends on who you talk to. If you encounter one, I'd treat them with kid gloves. If they decide you're a threat, they react with sudden and extreme violence and they're very difficult to kill."

I drove straight home. Of course, I hit a traffic jam on 45. A semi had overturned, clogging both lanes. The radio said no one was seriously hurt, but by the time I finally rolled into the garage, it was dark. The street was empty. Not a single leaf shivered on the old oak in the yard, its branches dripping midnight gloom onto the grass.

The house clanged at my approach, sliding the shutters and locks open. Beast shot out at my feet, dashed left, right, left, and overcome with excitement, zoomed around me in a circle, tucking her hind legs under her as she ran.

"I love you, too, you silly dog."

The doors opened and I stepped inside. The familiar smell of cinnamon floated around me, as the soft lamps came on one by one. I nodded at the portrait of my parents. The pressure that had accreted on my shoulders during the trip vanished. I was home.

I made a cup of coffee and sat in my chair in the lobby. Beast hopped onto my lap.

"Terminal, please."

The wall in front of me fractured, folded back on itself, and revealed the smooth surface of a screen.

"Audio."

Two long speakers emerged from the wall next to the screen.

"Camera footage since I've been gone."

The screen split into four different images. Cars. Two kids on bikes. Wind moving the oak branches. An older woman jogging past –I'd seen her before. She jogged by the house every afternoon, rain or shine. "Fast forward to activity."

The day turned into evening, rather than night. An image on the top left showed a dark figure at the edge of the inn. The timer said eleven twenty-two p.m.

"Enlarge."

The image expanded, taking over most of the screen. The inner camera took up the one third on the right. Sean Evans. He wore a gray T-shirt and loose jeans. He sniffed the air, turned, and looked straight at the camera. His eyes shone like two embers. Very deliberately he took a step forward onto the inn's grounds.

Just what I needed. I sat back and watched the video.

The recording from the inner camera produced a faint sound, a sigh, as the house creaked, preparing to defend itself.

Sean padded around the building, moving lightly on his toes.

On screen Beast dashed down the stairs and squeezed out through the dog door. The image of the outside expanded to cover the entire screen.

Beast paused on the porch for half a second, then sprinted, comically bounding down the stairs. She circled the house and stopped thirty feet from Sean.

He turned to her.

Beast bared little white teeth and barked.

"Look, dog, and I'm using the word dog loosely here. You and I aren't going to have a problem."

Beast barked again, pretending to lunge forward and backing up.

"Go away," Sean said. "Shoo. I don't want to hurt you."

He was sizing up the back door. He must've decided it was the easiest point of entry.

Beast barked again.

"Yeah, whatever." Sean took a step toward the house.

Beast growled. The undertone of her growl changed, gaining a vicious edge. Sean squinted at her.

Beast's long fur stood up like hackles on a cat. Claws slid from her feet. Her mouth gaped, wider and wider, as if her entire head had split in half. Four rows of fangs gleamed inside.

"What the hell...?" Sean backed away.

Beast jumped, covering ten feet in a single leap.

Sean grabbed a young oak branch and jerked it off the tree. Beast launched herself and he swung the branch like a bat, trying to knock her aside. With a sound somewhere between an upset wolverine and a pissed-off bobcat, Beast clamped on to the branch. Sean jerked it back and forth, trying to get her loose. Beast hung on and went airborne. Four rows of teeth crushed the wood –chomp-chomp-chomp –and Sean stumbled back, a stump of a branch in his hand.

Beast landed on her paws and bared her fangs. "Awwwwreeeeeoo!"

"Oh shit."

Sean spun around and ran to the nearest apple tree. Beast howled again and gave chase. He jumped and scrambled up the trunk and into the branches. Beast zoomed around the tree, barking her head off.

Sean braced his legs against the split in the trunk, looking comfortable. Beast sprinted around the trunk, circling it left, then right, in a black-and-white blur.

Sean bared his teeth and snarled. Even watching it on video, the hair on the back of my neck rose. It was the sound of a large, terrifying predator –hungry, savage, and confident –and it touched off some instinctual fear that made me glad to be inside my house with the lights on and doors locked.

A normal dog would've taken off. Beast barked at him, bouncing up and down in the grass.

"Can't climb, huh?" Sean asked in a deep, raspy voice. His eyes shone like two yellow moons. "Too bad."

Beast zoomed around the tree again, stopped, and bit the trunk.

"Quit it!"

She dashed away from the trunk, reversed on a dime, and bit the tree again. Wood chips littered the grass.

"I said quit it! I don't want to hurt you."

"Awwreeeeeeoo. Bark-bark-bark!" She bit the tree and chomped at the wood, spinning around the trunk like a whirlwind of teeth and fur. The tree shuddered.

Sean swore, plucked a small unripe apple from the tree, took aim, and dropped it on her head.

Beast howled in outrage.

He grabbed another apple and hurled it like a baseball. It hit the ground inches from her. She leaped back. A barrage of apples pounded the grass. Beast zigzagged like a running back with a football in his hands.

Sean leapt from the tree and sprinted in the opposite direction with inhuman speed. Beast gave chase, a streak of black and white. The camera turned as far as it could, tracking them to the edge of the property, but they vanished from view. A moment later Beast trotted back, climbed the steps, squirmed through the dog door, and collapsed on the rug, exhausted.

I cuddled her up. "Best dog ever."

Beast rubbed her face against my shirt and licked me.

"I think it's time for some treats." I got up, went to the kitchen, and took out a plastic container with beef ribs, which I'd bought specifically for that purpose. The Shih Tzu danced around my feet. I pulled a rib out and offered it to her. Beast grabbed it and took it under the table, making happy monster-dog noises.

I snapped the lid back on the container and put it in the fridge. Sean would be back. I was sure of it.

Somehow in a space of forty-eight hours, my life had gotten seriously complicated. I sighed and washed my hands. I was too tired to think. The X-ray of the stalker's body would have to wait till the morning.

CHAPTER FIVE

I stared at the X-ray image of the stalker's body. I might as well have tried to put together a thousand-piece puzzle with all the corner pieces missing. Apparently stalkers formed small bony plates in their tissues. For what purpose, I had no idea. The plates dappled the X-ray like scales on a python, and beneath this chaotic mess strange bones formed weird patterns. I had gone down to the lab as soon as I woke up and I'd been there for two hours. I hadn't been able to find the tracker. I'd tried magnets; I'd tried X-ray; I'd even tried searching for radiation, electromagnetic waves, and magic. Nothing.

No-thing. I had a body with a possible transmitter somewhere in it, which could even now be broadcasting its location to a lethal creature possibly camping in Avalon Subdivision, and I couldn't find it.

The magic splashed against me, urgent and sudden. Speak of the devil. Someone just entered the inn grounds.

I pulled my gloves off and grabbed my broom. I was getting tired of the game. If this dahaka thought the inn was an easy target, he was sorely mistaken.

I ran up the stairs, letting them seal behind me, and to the front door, toward the source of disturbance.

The body of a stalker lay ten feet from the boundary of the inn. Unlike my corpse, this one had reddish fur and it sprawled right in the middle of the sidewalk. In plain sight. At ten o'clock in the morning. It didn't look like a dead dog. It didn't look like a dead deer. It looked like some out-of-this-world monstrosity, which is exactly what it was, and in precisely five minutes Mr. Ramirez would be rounding the bend of this sidewalk, walking his Rhodesian Ridgeback, Asad, just as he had every day for the three years I had lived here.

This was probably a trap. It didn't matter. I had to get the stalker onto the inn grounds before anyone saw it.

I sprinted across the yard. The beast lay on its side, its head turned almost completely around. Bones protruded from the torn flesh on its neck. Something had snapped its neck and then ripped out its throat for a good measure.

No time to bother with hooks or spears. I dropped the broom on the grass, ran into the street, grabbed the stalker's legs, and pulled. The body slid across concrete. Heavy. I strained and pulled it in short jerks across the sidewalk. One, two, three...

Magic tinged through me –another intruder. I jerked the body onto the grass, behind the firecracker bush, and spun around. Sean Evans winked at me. He was holding my broom.

Oh, you idiot.

Sean moved. I sort of saw it –a blur rushed toward me and then I was pinned to the oak. His big body braced me, his left leg pressing mine to the tree, his left arm braced against the bark over my shoulder. He leaned into me, holding the broom out of my reach with his right hand and grinning a happy, self-satisfied wolf grin.

"What are you going to do now, tough guy?"

Our faces were mere inches apart. His amber eyes laughed at me. A tiny electric zing ran through me. He was entirely too close.

He studied my face and nodded at the broom. "Is this your broom? Yes? I've got what you want, buttercup."

He had what I wanted, huh. Buttercup, huh. Okay. "You sure seem happy with yourself," I said.

"Of course I am. I took you by surprise, took away your toy, and I've trapped you against this tree. I think we'll start with an apology."

"Me? Apologize to you? For what?"

"For trying to kill me by throwing me against the tree. Also, we need to have a conversation about your little dog."

I looked into his eyes. "Sean…"

"Yes?" He leaned even closer and he was looking at me with a kind of distinctly male fascination. What do you know? I'd caught the werewolf's eye. Lucky me. I sent a magic pulse toward the broom. The top of the broom handle melted, forming a bubble of gray metal streaked through with bright blue veins. Now I just had to keep his gaze off it.

I looked into the wolf's eyes. "I've never considered killing you."

"Aha."

"But now I'm tempted."

He smiled. The smile lit his face, giving him a dangerous, wicked edge, and… humor. He knew he was bad. He thought it was funny. Wow. I've never before understood the true meaning of "handsome devil." I knew logically what it meant, but now I saw it in action. Sean was a handsome devil in the flesh: arrogant, dangerous, and hot. I knew he was bad for me, but I had this absurd pull to reach out and touch his face. If he weren't so happy with himself, I might have even considered it.

"I've got your broom and you're not going anywhere," Sean said. "I'd like to see you try."

"You sure about that?"

"Yeah. Give it your best shot."

I pushed. The bubble of metal chomped on Sean's fist, fusing it to the broom. His eyes went wide. I patted his shoulder. "Take him inside and hold him." The broom jerked him back and dragged him across the grass. The house doors swung open like the cavernous mouth of a colossal beast, gulped Sean down, then closed.

"Take the body to the lab and seal it," I murmured.

The earth beneath the stalker gaped and swallowed the corpse.

I pulled my T-shirt down, straightening it. Mr. Ramirez walked by. His dog sniffed at the sidewalk.

"Good morning!" I called out.

Mr. Ramirez nodded in a solemn way. "Good morning. Nice day today."

"I heard we might reach a hundred degrees."

"Heat is good for an old man like me."

I smiled. "Oh, Mr. Ramirez, you're not old."

"I am, but the alternative is worse." He waved at me and went on his way.

I turned and strode to the house. Sean was stuck to a wall like a fly to the flypaper. The broom had melted into dozens of narrow, elastic metal filaments that stretched across Sean's body, holding him tight and pulsing with blue every time he tried to break free. Smooth wooden roots as thick as my arm curved around his limbs, melting back into the wall. The house had decided to get in on the action. Only Sean's face was clearly visible, but his eyes told me he was determined to find a way to free himself.

Caldenia descended down the stairs and saw him. "Ooo. Planning a kinky morning?"

"No, just dealing with a pesky intruder."

"Oh well. If you kill him, do save me his liver. Werewolf liver is a very tender delicacy." She licked her lips. "Especially when sautéed in butter."

"What the hell…?" Sean growled.

"I'll keep that in mind."

Caldenia walked past me to the kitchen, took a bag of Funyuns off the counter, then headed back upstairs.

I closed the distance between Sean and me and crossed my arms. "Now then. We have to talk."

Sean studied me, his amber eyes completely lucid. "So it's not the broom."

"No." It was me.

His eyes narrowed. "But you didn't use any of your awesome powers to grab that corpse off the road. Whatever it is, it's limited to the house."

Sean Evans might have been crazy, but he wasn't stupid.

"You're not the first werewolf I've met," I told him.

"Meaning what?"

"Meaning I'm not buying your growly act. You're designed to maintain calm while under heavy fire and you haven't once lost your temper. Even when I threw you against the tree. Which was accidental, by the way. I would never do that to one of my trees on purpose."

He flashed his teeth at me. "See, you shouldn't give away targets like that. Next time I want to piss you off, I'll just have to cut down a couple of your saplings."

"You haven't shifted into wetwork shape. Also, you're methodically testing your restraints while showing me your big teeth and pretending to snarl at me."

"I haven't really tested them yet," Sean said.

That I could believe. "Good, because I haven't used any of my power to hold you yet. Right now all that's restraining you is the house and the broom. I can get involved, but I would much rather talk."

Sean considered it. "Fine. Let's talk. Whatever powers you have are limited to the house, and I can tell by looking at you that you're a civilian. You don't have the right muscle tone, and you don't move like someone who has experience cutting at living bodies in close quarters. You aren't one hundred percent sure what you're dealing with or you know exactly what you're dealing with, but either way you're scared."

"And how did you figure that out?"

"Yesterday you left early in the morning and didn't come back until late. I saw your face when you went to your car. You stopped and looked at the house. You looked worried. The old lady, who normally sits on that balcony for hours, spent the entire day inside."

"You were watching my house."

"Yes. Those things out there, whatever the hell they are, aren't playing around. You expected them to attack the house, which is why you warned your tenant to hide. There is only one reason why someone in your position would leave for a long trip. You went for help. Doesn't look to me like you got it."

Underestimating him was a really bad idea. "And how did you deduce that, Mr. Holmes?"

He smiled. "Elementary, Watson. If you'd found help, you'd be more upbeat. Instead when you got out of your car, you looked like you were dragging an anchor behind you. I've seen that look before. It's the look that says 'I radioed for air support and they told me none will be coming and another enemy battalion is heading my way.'" He tilted his head. "You may not have the air support, but you have me."

"Wait a minute. Just yesterday some man barged into my house and ranted about handling everything himself. Was that you?"

"Yesterday I thought you were just a normal person and I didn't want to see you hurt. Dina, you're forcing me to split my attention. I'm reasonably certain you're safe in your house, but you keep leaving that safety. I can't patrol the neighborhood and babysit you at the same time, and since you haven't been forthcoming with information, I never know when you're going on another expedition into the subdivision. I have to sit here on my hands like a little kid and watch your house. I don't like sitting on my hands."

"I didn't ask for your protection."

"You did ask me to do something about the dead dogs."

He had me there.

"I've spent years being dragged halfway around the world and fighting because someone told me to do it. I chose this place to settle down. This is my territory as your house is your territory. This is home. I will fight for it. And for the record, I never intended to let the dog killings slide."

"And if I don't want your protection?"

Sean looked at me like I wasn't right in the head. "As I said, your house is in my territory. I will keep you safe."

Right. He was genetically engineered to withstand sieges and guard things against overwhelming odds. He probably couldn't overcome the protective impulse even if he wanted to, and he definitely didn't want to. "Aren't you too young to be guarding the gate, Sean?"

He frowned. "I don't follow."

Maybe he really didn't know. "I'm an innkeeper. Does that mean anything to you?"

He chuckled. "I hate to break it to you, but you own a bed-and-breakfast and your only guest seems to be a freaky old woman. Calling yourself an innkeeper is a stretch if you catch my drift."

He had no clue what I was talking about. "How about Auul? Does that ring a bell?"

When pronounced the right way, the name rhymed with Raul, but it was softer, said with more longing, each vowel stretched until it sounded like the howl of a lonely wolf under the full moon.

"Cute," he said. "Are you going to bark at me next? I don't mind being mocked, but I'd like to keep this conversation productive."

I pushed with my magic. "Terminal, Auul file, please."

The house shivered. A big screen formed on the far wall. On it a vast forest spread, viewed from above, a place of giants. Enormous trees with blue-green leaves shimmered in the night breeze, and above them midnight sky reigned, sprayed with sparkling stars that glittered like jewels. An enormous moon rose on the right, taking up a quarter of the horizon, glowing with blue and green, and past it the second moon, an intense gold shot through with red, hung in the distance. An enormous bird, the tips of its feathers glowing with pale blue, flew above the treetops.

Sean strained. His eyes lit up, catching the light. Muscles bunched under the strands. The elastic metal cords snapped and he stepped from the wall, staring at the image.

Wow. I let him go —there was no point in holding him. The torn metal ligaments melted, dripped down, and flowed across the floor toward me, reshaping themselves. They surged up and a broom handle touched my hand. I took it.

"Auul," I quoted. "Soft like the whisper of love on a mother's lips, harsh like a cry for vengeance, you are a memory, a child's dream, a debt still owed, watered with our blood, lost forever but never forgotten."

"Who wrote that?" Sean asked, his gaze still fixed on the image.

"A werewolf. Your kind got very poetic about your planet after you blew it up."

Sean turned to me. "My *planet?* I was born in Tennessee."

"Where do werewolves come from?"

"We were always here. We're a genetic mutation, an abnormality. Where does your broom come from?"

Aha. "Tell me this image doesn't call to you, Sean."

He looked at the moon again.

The image melted, replaced by a lean woman with fiery eyes. Her hair spilled over her back in a long reddish mane, held back by gold hair clasps. Delicate metal lace sheathed her shoulders. A narrow gold chain ran under her uncovered breasts. Music came, quiet, haunting, and she began to sway, her long, diaphanous dark skirt flaring as she turned. She sang in a dead language and Sean listened to it as if he understood every word.

The woman finished her song. The file said it was a lullaby. I wondered if Sean had heard it in childhood.

"Okay," he said finally. "Hit me with it."

"You won't like it."

"Why don't you let me decide that?"

He did ask. I would remind him of that if he freaked out.

"There is a star system with two habitable planets, Auul and Mraar." The image changed, pulling the image of the two planets out of the file. "It's not clear if Auul was habitable at the start or terraformed. Everyone agrees that civilization began on Mraar. If you ask the Sun Horde, a splinter group occupied Auul and declared independence. If you ask your people, they were exiled to Auul and abandoned. We don't know what the truth is, and we never will. Everyone does agree that after the civilizations had existed independently for almost a thousand years, the Raoo of Mraar invaded Auul."

I sat in the chair. I was tired of standing.

"How do you know this?" Sean asked.

"I'm an innkeeper."

"That explains nothing, but okay. What happened with invasion?"

"The Raoo got their butts kicked. It's difficult to occupy a planet."

"Makes sense in theory. Getting enough troops to the surface would be a challenge."

He was taking all this rather well. He probably thought I was crazy and had decided to stay calm in case I started putting tinfoil on my head.

"The war dragged on for years, really more a cycle of invasions and hasty retreats, until the Raoo acquired a gate. Whether someone sold them the technology or they stumbled on it, we don't know. Most likely they bought it somehow."

"What's a gate?"

"It's an Einstein-Rosen bridge. A miniature traversable wormhole, which permits nearly instantaneous travel from one part of the universe to another. There are naturally occurring wormholes, but the Raoo built a synthetic one. It took a huge amount of energy to keep it running, and it could only be active for a short time or it would destabilize the planet. In the fourteen days it was open, the Raoo dumped millions of their troops on Auul. Mraar was overcrowded and Auul had always been sparsely populated. Your people were losing. With two-thirds of the planet occupied, they resorted to drastic measures and engineered werewolfism. They proceeded to administer it to every citizen, raised a new generation of superfighters, and the tide of war began to turn."

"Back up." Sean held his hand out. "What do you mean engineered?"

"They created an *ossai*, an artificial microscopic programmable virus. They loaded it with a program and used it to rewrite the genetic code of living organisms. Once it was administered, the ossai made the current generation stronger and faster and reshaped their offspring into werewolves. When you change shape it must hurt, but it doesn't hurt as much as it should. That's because when you change, the ossai in your body releases a painkiller."

"I've been in the military," Sean said. "I've had a lot of blood tests."

"The ossai is tiny. It also self-destructs when removed from the body. Cursory tests wouldn't detect it, so unless someone sequences your genetic code, you will pass for a native."

He grimaced. "Never mind. What happened with the invasion?"

"It took the Raoo almost a century, but eventually they reverse engineered the ossai and made their own version, bigger, better, badder –the werecats, also known as the Sun Horde. Your people had anticipated that this would happen because by the time the Sun Horde emerged, they were already building their own gates. The decision was made to abandon Auul, but your people didn't want the Mraar to have it. They left the gates opened, knowing it would lead to a catastrophe, and evacuated as much of the population as they could to other places in the universe. It took years. To hold the gates against the incoming Sun Horde, they bred a second generation of werewolves, which has been described to me as more powerful but less stable, to which you apparently belong."

"Nice," Sean said.

"The alpha strain werewolves held the gates as long as they could until finally their operation created a tiny black hole. The black hole consumed the planet, releasing enormous amounts of energy, until Auul was completely gone. The resulting cataclysm created a very small but super-dense mass, which upset the balance within the star system, rendering Mraar uninhabitable. Some of the Sun Horde got out, but not many. The death count was in the billions. Now Mraar is a dead rock and Auul is an asteroid belt. The people of both are refugees on the known worlds."

I waved the broom and the screen disappeared.

"That's an interesting story," Sean said. "So according to this creative narrative, when did all this happen?"

"The werewolves have been visiting Earth for centuries," I said. "Some via other gates, some by different means. But the last refugees from Auul arrived here forty-two years ago."

Most people would've told me I was insane by now. Sean was calm like a rock.

Beast ran down the stairs, leaped into my lap, and showed him her teeth.

He bared his own teeth at her. "I'll deal with you later." He looked at me. "I need to make a phone call. Do you mind?"

I nodded at the back door. "The porch is all yours."

He went out. The screen door shut behind him, and I heard his muted voice. "Hey, Dad. It's me. Does the word Auul mean anything to you?"

CHAPTER SIX

Beast and I watched from the inside of the inn as Sean paced back and forth. He was talking to his parents and it wasn't going well.

"Aha. Were you ever going to tell me? ... When did you think I would be old enough? I'm a grown goddamned man, Dad. I've fought in two wars. ... No, sir, I'm not being disrespectful, I'm angry. ... I do have a right to be angry. You lied to me. ... Not telling the whole story is still lying, Dad. It's lying by omission. ... I think we're doing a fine job discussing this over the phone. ... Yes, please, do put me on speaker. ... Hey, Mom. ... Yes. ... Yes. ... No, I'm not upset. ... A girl. ... No, you can't talk to her."

And now I was involved. I could just imagine how that conversation would go. "Yes, hi, who are you and how do you know so much about werewolves and what exactly is your relationship with my son..."

"An innkeeper."

Now what?

Sean walked down the steps, heading deeper into the orchard. I strained. His lips were moving, but he was out of my earshot.

I sighed and looked at Beast. She licked my hand. Sean was getting a crash course in inns and innkeepers and I had no clue what they were telling him.

Ten minutes later Sean put away his phone, came back inside, and landed in a chair.

"So, how did it go?"

"About as well as you think it did." He leaned against the chair and exhaled. "They both were in their twenties when they came over here, enlisted in the Army, and built a new life. They didn't tell me because apparently our particular second-generation kind isn't welcome among other Auul refugees, and they didn't want me to have a chip on my shoulder."

A chip? Now he was carrying a two-by-four.

Sean fixed me with his stare. Uh-oh.

"How does the broom work?"

"Magic."

He locked his jaw. "Don't give me that. You hit me with the planets and wormholes. You cracked the door open. Might as well just swing it wide."

No, he cracked the door open with his midnight marking expedition. I petted Beast. "Have you ever heard of Arthur C. Clarke's third law of prediction? It states that any sufficiently advanced technology is indistinguishable from magic. Take a smart phone and hand it to an ancient Roman. He'll think it's a magic window into the world of the gods and that the Beyoncé video playing on it is showing him Venus. The broom is magic. The inn is magic. I'm magic. I can feel it, I can manipulate it, but I can't explain it. You've transformed hundreds of times in your life under the belief that it's magic. Why does it matter now that it's not?"

Sean drummed his fingers on the armrest of his chair. "So this place is supposed to be a sanctuary?"

"Yes and no. It's an inn, a neutral ground. An abnormality in the ordinary reality of this planet or whatever passes for it. I'm an innkeeper. Here I'm supreme. If you are accepted as a guest, you fall under my protection and as long as you stay here, you will enjoy the right of sanctuary. For various reasons, Earth is a way station for many travelers. We're the Atlanta of the galaxy: many beings stop here for a layover. Some are alien and some are not. The innkeepers maintain the order, provide them with a safe place to stay, and minimize the population exposure and the bloodbath that could result. Nobody wants a worldwide panic. It has been so for hundreds of years."

"So the old lady is a guest?"

"Yes."

"How long will she be staying?"

"She paid for a lifetime stay."

"Clever." Sean leaned forward. "So she stays in your inn and nobody can get her out. What did she do?"

"You don't want to know."

"You're not going to tell me."

I shook my head. "No." I protected my guests and that included safeguarding their privacy.

Sean pondered me. I could almost feel the wheels turning in his head. He was disturbingly quick on the uptake.

"My father told me that, as an innkeeper, you're supposed to remain neutral."

"It's customary that I do. There is no compulsion or law that forces me to maintain my neutrality."

"And you can't ask for help."

"Your father is wrong. It's up to each innkeeper's discretion whether or not to ask a guest or a third party for assistance. Most innkeepers never resort to such requests because we don't want to put others in danger. The safety of our guests is our first priority."

Sean smiled. Under ordinary circumstances, I might have enjoyed seeing it –he was really handsome –but the way he was smiling now made me want to turn my broom into a shield, preferably with spikes, and brace myself.

"So you asked me for help and now I'm in danger because of it."

What? "I did no such thing. At no point did the words 'Help me, Sean Evans' come out of my mouth."

Beast barked to underscore my point.

"You approached me" –he counted off on his fingers –" you admonished me for my inaction, you tried to elicit an assurance that I would do something about the situation, and then, after I assured you I would, you still involved yourself in a violent action, escalating the level of danger for both of us. All of this can be construed as a plea for assistance and cooperation, and now because of you, my life is in jeopardy."

"No." This was crazy. There were so many things I wanted to say at once if the words would just get out of each other's way.

"Fine." He grinned again, flashing white teeth. "Is there someone we can contact and settle this dispute? Somebody with the power of oversight, perhaps?"

The Innkeeper Assembly. Oh, you bastard. His father must've told him about it. "Are you threatening me?"

"I don't make threats. I solve problems."

"And that didn't sound conceited. Not at all."

He spread his arms. "I'm simply stating facts."

The Assembly was an informal self-governing organization of innkeepers. If Sean went to them, their investigation would begin and end with one question: *"Was the inn directly threatened?"* I would have to answer no. Technically I hadn't broken any written laws because we didn't have any, but I'd broken the unspoken canon of neutrality. They would view it as unwise, advise me to not do it again, and bump the rating of the inn down to one mark, which would broadcast to everyone that staying at Gertrude Hunt equaled gambling with your safety. The inn was at already at two marks due to having been abandoned and me being an unknown commodity. My parents' inn had been rated at five. Getting branded with one mark would kill any chances of reviving Gertrude Hunt. We would not recover.

Argh. He had me and he knew it. "Just what exactly did your parents do in the military?"

"My dad was arrested once because he didn't know the laws, so he decided he would learn all of them. He went green to gold, which means he became an officer and worked as a JAG Corps attorney. My mother really enjoyed watching people's heads explode from far away, so she served as a countersniper."

Great. "What do you want?"

"I want us to work together."

"So let me get this straight. First, I ask you to work together and you refuse, then you invade my property, make fun of me, attempt to intimidate me, attack my dog..."

"I think calling her a dog is a stretch."

"Her ancestors were Shih Tzus, so technically she's a canine derivative. You attack my dog..."

"She chased me up a tree!"

Beast growled.

"You deserved it. Where was I?"

"Dog," he said helpfully.

"Yes. You attack my dog, then you attack me in the yard, and now you're blackmailing me into cooperating. Wouldn't it have been easier to just work with me when I asked you to?"

He pointed at himself. "First, lone wolf. I work alone. That's my natural setting. Second, I thought you were just a normal person who somehow knew about werewolves. I didn't have all the relevant information. Had I known you had a haunted house, a magic broom, and a devil dog on your side, my initial response would've been different."

I crossed my arms.

"I'm sorry for intimidating you," he said. "I'm sorry if I scared you."

"You didn't."

"Well, I'm sorry in any case. Like it or not, you asked me for help, and now we're in this together. It's in your best interest and mine to nuke these assholes as soon as possible. You know more about what's going on, but I can kill them faster and cleaner than you can."

That was true, but I didn't have to like it.

"If you work with me, I promise I won't keep secrets from you, and I will take your opinion into consideration before I act. I also promise not to seek revenge on the small demon in your lap for a completely unprovoked attack."

Beast growled and he smiled. It was a disarming, boyish smile. The wolf was still in his eyes, but now he pretended very hard that he was just a small fluffy puppy. "What do you say?"

I didn't want him going to the Assembly. I had a feeling he wouldn't, but the risk was there and I couldn't ignore it. And, setting that aside, I needed help. Werewolf kind of help. Which is why I had approached him in the first place.

"Dina?"

And he had to stop saying my name in that voice. "I'm wondering if I should make you grovel more."

"That's probably all the groveling you're going to get. If you say no, I'll go for it by myself. It will be messy and ugly."

I exhaled. There was no point in fighting with him anymore. "How's your sense of smell?"

"Acute."

"Do you think you could smell a foreign object inside one of these creatures?"

Sean blinked. "I'll give it a shot."

"Okay. We work together. But only until this is over. And if you betray my trust, I will banish you out of this inn. I mean it, Sean. You have my word that it won't be gentle. You won't like it, and it will take you a long time to find your way back to your house."

I had two options. I could bring Sean into my lab under the house or I could bring the body of the stalker to him. The first involved letting him into my private place where I stored books and other things. Typically guests were not allowed in the lab and for a good reason. The second involved rearranging the architecture of the inn.

I wasn't ready to let him into the lab. I wasn't ready to let him see what I could really do inside the inn either, but that seemed like a lesser evil at this point.

I tapped the floor with the broom, letting my magic stream through it and down into the floor, into the walls, into the laboratory table below us. I pushed. Wood and metal flowed like molten wax. A long, narrow fissure formed in the floor of the living room. The wood dripped down, the hole widened, and the lab table emerged, complete with the body of the stalker on it, still secured with metal restraints. I had tried to autopsy it, and the front of it lay open, the skin pinned aside with surgical clamps. I wasn't quite sure what the stalker's inner organs were supposed to look like, but my spear had done a number on its insides, and currently it was a mess of torn tissue.

Dry tissue. Its blood had evaporated despite me sealing it in plastic.

"Son of a bitch." Sean stared at the table. "What else can this place do?"

"Wouldn't you like to know?"

"Yes, I would."

"How about you sniff out the tracker instead?"

Sean circled the body. "I know you stabbed it at least twenty times."

"How?"

"Well, the fact that its internal organs are a mess is a clue, but I went down to the Quirks' place once the cops left. There are scratches on the brick of the eastern wall, the kind a bladed weapon makes. So what did you use?"

He didn't miss much. "A spear."

Sean bent closer to the body. His nostrils flared.

"Well? What's your professional opinion?"

"A few years ago, our unit came home from a tour of duty in an ugly place. For the whole last month of that tour, a buddy of mine, Jason Thomas, was talking about how he would get home and eat a hotdog. He wanted a hotdog with everything on it. So we get home, we go out that night, and he gets himself two hotdogs with everything on them. Then we hit the bars and he goes straight for Jose Cuervo. Long story short, two hours later he threw up in an alley."

"And?"

"My professional opinion is that this smells just like that hotdog-tequila vomit."

Ha. Ha. "I could've told you that and I'm not a werewolf."

Sean took another whiff. "Look, I've smelled decomposing bodies before. Human bodies, animal bodies. This smells wrong. Where is it from, because it's not from around here."

"It's from some hellish corner of the universe I know pretty much nothing about."

"What am I smelling for? Metal, plastic, what?"

"I don't know."

Sean inhaled again. "The carcass is too acrid. Metal and plastic don't give off strong scents. If there's something in there, the stench is blocking it."

"So far you're not much help."

"Dina, I don't even know what I'm looking for."

He had a point. I wasn't being fair. I was being snippy too, and it really had nothing to do with Sean and everything to do with me being frustrated. "Would an X-ray help?"

"You X-rayed it?"

I raised my hand. The X-ray slid through the floor and I held it out to Sean. He lifted it to the window, letting the light shine through the film. "What the hell…?"

"That's what I said." I sat in the chair. "I've tried magnets. I've scanned it for magic emissions, radio signal, radiation, and I went over it with a voltage detector just in case. Nothing."

"Are you sure it even has a tracker?"

"No."

Sean pondered me. "How about starting at the beginning?"

I explained about dahaka and stalkers and the now-destroyed inn.

Sean frowned. "So wait a minute, someone destroyed that inn and your Assembly didn't do anything about it?"

I shook my head. "No. Each innkeeper is on his or her own. The Assembly just sets policies and rates the inns, kind of like a cosmic Triple A. If someone walks in here and kills me, they'll do nothing about it. If you went to them complaining about me, they'd just rate my inn unsafe, which means nobody would stay here."

"So I would be taking away your livelihood."

The way he said it suggested he felt guilty about it. Huh. What do you know, a werewolf with a conscience. "Not only that, but an inn is a living entity. It forms a symbiotic relationship with its guests. Without guests, the inn will weaken and fall dormant, almost like a bear slipping into hibernation. If the inn stays dormant for too long, it will wither and die."

The house creaked around me, the thick timbers in its wall groaning in alarm.

"There is no chance of that happening," I told it. "You have me and you have Caldenia."

"Is it sentient?" Sean peered at the walls.

"The house understands some things. I don't know if it's sentient in the way you and I are, but it's definitely a living thing, Sean."

Caldenia walked through the door. She was carrying a tomato vine with four ripe, red tomatoes on it. Caldenia saw the stalker's body. Her carefully shaped eyebrows rose.

Now what? "Yes, Your Grace?"

"I'm glad that after months of a perfectly boring existence, the inn is now a hotbed of interesting activity. I do have to tell you that the reek is abominable. What are you doing?"

"We're trying to determine if this corpse has a tracking device somewhere inside it."

"Ah. Have fun, but before you dig into it, look at this."

She showed me the tomatoes.

"I just had a perfectly lovely conversation with the woman who lives down the street. Her name is Emily, I believe."

"Mrs. Ward?"

Caldenia waved her fingers. "Yes, something or other. Apparently she grows tomatoes in her backyard."

"Did you go off the inn grounds?"

"Of course not, dear, I'm not an imbecile. We spoke over the hedge. I would like to grow tomatoes."

Whatever kept her occupied. "Very well. I'll purchase some plants and gardening tools."

"Also a hat," Caldenia said. "One of those hideous straw affairs with little flowers on them."

"Of course."

"I'm going to grow green tomatoes, and then we'll fry them in butter."

"Your Grace, you've never tried fried green tomatoes."

"Life is about new experiences." Caldenia gave me a toothy smile.

"I'd eat it," Sean said.

I stared at him.

He shrugged. "They're good."

"You blackmailed me. You are not invited for these theoretical fried tomatoes."

"Nonsense," Caldenia said. "They're my theoretical tomatoes. You are invited."

I sighed. That was all I could do.

Caldenia headed up the stairs and stopped. "By the way. Back in my younger days, a man broke into my estate and stole the Star of Inndar. It was a beautiful jewel, light blue and excellent for storing light-recorded data. I was keeping my financial records on it. I'd thought the man was perhaps a revolutionary come to heroically overthrow my rule, but sadly he was just an ordinary thief motivated by money. He was a karian, and he'd hidden dozens of pouches in his flesh. Before he was captured, he'd hidden the Star somewhere in his body. I required the jewel that evening to complete a certain financial agreement, and I didn't have time to dig through him and risk damaging the Star in the process."

"So what did you do?" Sean said.

Never ask that question.

"I boiled him, my dear. It is still the only sure way to separate hard bits from all that flesh. And you have the added advantage of your captive being already dead, so there will be none of those annoying screams to alert the neighborhood. Good luck."

She went up the stairs.

Sean looked at me. "Is she for real?"

"Very much so." I looked at the body. "If we try to boil it, there's no telling what sort of gasses or poisons it will release. We'll have to vent it outside, and it's going to stink." And it will be the kind of stench that would cause the whole neighborhood to call 911.

Sean thought about it. "Is that smoker I saw on the back porch okay to use?"

"Probably. Are you suggesting we smoke it?" What in the world...

"No, I am suggesting we smoke a side of pork ribs. With lots and lots of hickory wood."

The stalker's body sprawled on the table like some grotesque butterfly straight out of a drug-induced nightmare. Although most of the blood had evaporated, it still had to weigh close to a hundred pounds. We'd have to take it apart.

"Do you have a really large pot?" Sean asked.

"Follow me."

I led him into the kitchen and to the door of my pantry, located a couple of cabinets away from the refrigerator. Sean leaned back out of the kitchen doorway, checked the wall width –it was a regular six-inch wall –and leaned back. "Follow you where? Into the closet?"

Oh, you chucklehead. I opened the door and flicked the light on. Five hundred square feet of pantry space greeted Sean. Nine rows of shelves lined the walls, all the way to the nine-foot ceiling. Pots and pans filled the front shelves, and past them flour, sugar, and other dry goods waited in large plastic containers, each with a small label. A large chest freezer stood on the right against the wall.

Sean surveyed the pantry, turned on his foot, went to check the wall again, and came back. "How?"

I waved my fingers at him. "Magic."

"But…"

"Magic, Sean." I walked in and pulled the enormous sixty-quart pot from the shelf in the corner. "I have several of those."

"Where did you get all this stuff?"

"Before this inn was orphaned, it was a thriving place. Many guests meant a lot of large meals. The question now is how will we boil the bodies? I'm not too wild about having them in my kitchen. I suppose we can get some electric hotplates, set them on the back patio on the slab, and put the pots on top of that."

"Mhm." Sean didn't seem convinced. "Would it be hot enough, that's the question."

"We might have to take that chance. We want low heat anyway."

He smirked at me. "Boiled many bodies, have you?"

"No, but I've made a lot of pulled pork."

"Sixty quarts is a lot of water to heat."

"What's the alternative?"

"Let me think about it," Sean said. "I'm off to Home Depot, then. I should be back in an hour. Do I need to pick up some pork ribs?"

"No." I opened the chest freezer. Sean stared at a three-foot-high tower of pork rib sides vacuum sealed in plastic. I'd stacked them up like cordwood.

Sean struggled to process the ribs. Clearly he had been slapped with one surprise too many today.

"Okay," he said finally. "I'll bite. Why?"

"Beast likes to eat them."

"That explains it." He turned to the door.

"Sean, how much money do you need?"

He gave me a flat look. No outrage, no anger, just a wall of no. "I'll be back in an hour." He went out the door.

Hell would bloom before Sean Evans started taking care of my bills. I'd make him take the money. I just had to be smart about it.

I looked at Beast. "I'm having serious doubts about our partnership."

Beast didn't answer.

I still had to do something about the stalker bodies. Folding them in half wouldn't do it. They still wouldn't fit. I picked up my broom and pushed my magic. The metal flowed, folding itself into a razor-sharp machete blade.

This would get messy.

Fifty-two minutes later, I heard a truck. The magic boomed as the vehicle came up my driveway... and kept going, around the house, rolling over my grass until it stopped at my back patio.

I strode to the back door. It opened for me and I stepped out onto the porch. Beast followed me. An orange rental truck from Home Depot waited on the grass, parked so the truck bed faced me. It was filled with stacks of paver stones. Next to them rested bags of gravel, sand, a two-by-four, fireproof bricks... Sean hopped out of the front seat, opened the tailgate, and picked up two fifty-pound bags of sand without any apparent effort, as if they were jugs of milk.

"What happened to the hot-plate plan?"

"I did some thinking and one, it won't generate enough heat and two, we need additional fire to cover the stench."

"Aha."

"I checked the fire ordinance and it says all fire pits of this type should be twenty-five feet from any flammable structure. This patio is too close to the house, so I'm going to build you a new one."

I smiled at him and tapped the patio with my broom, sending a pulse of magic through it. The concrete slab rose out of the ground and slid over the grass. I put it about thirty feet out. "Far enough?"

Sean blinked.

"Sean?"

He recovered. "Sure. Saves me some work."

"Do you want help?"

"No, I got it."

"Suit yourself. I'll go make some lemonade then."

I went inside and sat at the bay window. Sean went over to the patio, looked at it for a while, then tested it with his boot. The patio predictably stayed where it was. Sean pondered it.

Oh, this was too good. I reached for the patio with my magic.

Sean stepped onto the concrete, putting his weight on the slab. The patio sank six inches into the ground. Sean jumped. He went straight up like a startled cat, twisted in the air, and landed on the grass. He-he! I raised the patio back up.

Sean took a step toward it. The patio slid back a foot. He took another step. The patio slid back again.

Sean spun to the house and saw me in the window. "Knock it off!"

I laughed and went to make the lemonade.

CHAPTER SEVEN

I used a spatula to rescue the last piece of French bread from the pan. I'd melted a bit of butter in a nonstick skillet and fried each piece until it turned golden brown. The trick wasn't getting the bread completely fried but instead just toasted enough for each slice to form a lovely golden crust.

I'd peeled some garlic cloves, so I took one, chopped the top off it, and began rubbing each slice of bread with the clove.

The first thing I'd done when I'd taken over the inn was update the kitchen with much larger windows, bring in new appliances, and replace the cracked and chipped white tile countertops. Money had been tight, so I'd gone with butcher block. The maple wood gave the kitchen a warm and inviting feel, and it was easier for the house to assimilate. Any building materials brought into the inn became part of the inn eventually. The inn could synthesize wood and stone, but it took a lot of energy, and providing it with the basics made things much easier. The inn fed on its environment, but the bulk of its life energy came from the guests and me. Without guests, it would fall dormant trying to conserve energy and when that happened, an inn decayed and fell apart just like any other house. When I had come to awaken Gertrude Hunt from its hibernation, it had been sleeping for so long, its siding had rotted away and a lot of the outside plumbing had succumbed to tree roots.

The day was in full swing, the afternoon golden and beautiful outside, and the countertops all but glowed as if glazed with honey. From my vantage point at the island, I could see the north patio facing the street. It was one of my favorite places to hang out. I'd sit in one of the canvas chairs and read my book.

Now the patio featured a smoker grill and Sean, armed with huge tongs. Beast lay by the grill. He'd bribed her with ribs.

I had to give it to him, the man knew how to build a fire. I kept the windows closed but even so, I could smell the spicy, tangy bite of hickory smoke. It smelled like childhood and it brought back the long, lazy summer days, barbecue, watermelon, and freeze pops. If I closed my eyes, I could almost convince myself it was Dad grilling outside rather than some werewolf with entitlement issues.

Best of all, the smoke drowned all other smells. Last night Sean had built an outdoor fire pit behind the house. He'd drawn a wide circle on the concrete, then built a wall of concrete blocks around it, leaving space to add wood. Next he lined the inside with fireproof bricks, leaving vent spaces, and installed the grill. We set the pots up, filled them with water from a hose, and let them cook through the night. The hickory chips in the fire pit drowned most of the stench, but if you stood right by the pot, you could smell an acrid, toxic odor. But to get to the back, any visitors would have to first pass by Sean's grill at the front of the house, and once they smelled the aroma of that barbecue, they wouldn't go any farther.

Sean raised the grill lid and checked the meat. He wore jeans and a plain green T-shirt. The T-shirt molded to his muscular shoulders. Sean had a peculiar kind of strength, powerful but lean, quick and supple, but without weakness. Like flexible steel.

And I've been looking at him entirely too long.

I finished with the bread, took a bowl with egg mixture out of the refrigerator, and started spreading it on the bread, arranging the slices on a pretty green platter as I went.

The screen door banged open and Sean sauntered into the kitchen. "What smells so good?"

How could he even smell it over the smoke? "Here, have one."

Sean snagged a sandwich off the platter and bit into it with a crunch. "Mmm. What's in this?"

"Egg, Miracle Whip, garlic, and French bread."

"So it's like an egg salad. It doesn't taste like an egg salad."

"That's because of the garlic and bread." I chopped green onion and sprinkled it on the sandwiches. "How are the ribs?"

"Good. We're about ready."

Sean reached for another sandwich. I raised my knife.

"Don't threaten me unless you mean to use it," he said.

"Don't steal food until it's served and I won't have to."

He laughed and went to wash his hands.

I took the lemonade and iced-tea pitchers to the table outside. Sean helped me bring out sandwiches, corn on the cob, napkins, and paper plates. Kayley Henderson and her boyfriend, Robbie, came down the sidewalk and stopped by the hedge.

"Are you the barbecue people?" Kayley asked.

"We are," I confirmed.

"We could smell it all the way from the bus stop." Robbie eyed the grill.

Sean emerged from inside. Kayley's eyebrows crept up.

"Why don't you join us," I said. "There's plenty to go around."

"Thank you!" Kayley chirped.

They came around and pulled up the chairs. A moment later Caldenia joined us.

Sean pulled the first rack of ribs off the grill and onto a wooden block. "Have to let them rest a bit."

Caldenia gifted Kayley with an inviting smile. "How are your studies going?"

For the next ten minutes we were entertained with stories of Cedar Creek High. Someone stole someone else's boyfriend, someone was selling their ADHD medication, and three boys were busted stealing the school flag. I wasn't that much older and things I'd been through would turn their hair white, but after hearing all that, I was really glad I was done with high school.

Sean carved the ribs and started passing them around the table. I cut a small piece from mine. It was delicious, just right, sweet and tangy with a hint of heat.

"Hey, you!" Margaret came up the street, her Pomeranian bouncing by her feet like a small fluff of fur. "Kayley, your mother is looking for you."

Kayley got up. "Can we take the food with us?"

I waved at them. "Please do."

"Thank you, Dina. The sandwiches are awesome."

The kids fled with their plates.

Misha ran around the hedge and Beast chased her, the two little dogs running in circles in the yard.

"Join us," Sean invited.

"Are you cooking for Dina?" Margaret opened her eyes wide. "Oooh."

"Don't they make a cute couple?" Caldenia said.

I resisted the urge to stab her with my fork. "We're not a couple. Sean fixed my smoker, so we decided to try it out."

"You're not cooking a dead body in there, are you?" Margaret asked.

I almost dropped my plate on my lap. "What? Eeew!"

Sean raised his eyebrows. "Why would you ask that?"

Margaret came around and sat in the chair. "You haven't seen the news? Turn on channel five."

Suddenly I got a cold nagging feeling that something was terribly wrong. I got up. "Excuse me a moment."

Sean followed me inside, into the front room.

"Screen," I said. "Channel five."

The wall opened, revealing the monitor. It came to life, showing footage of a rural house shot from above, likely from a helicopter.

"...Scene of a terrible tragedy," a male anchor's voice said. "What's the death count now, Amy?"

The footage switched to a blond reporter standing in front of a driveway. Behind her in the distance, the house loomed, flanked by police cars.

"Police officials confirmed that all forty-two cows were killed and partially eaten, Ryan. There is no official word on the condition of John Rook's body; however, sources close to the investigation tell us that he suffered the same fate as his livestock."

"Are you saying someone fed on his body?"

Amy looked like she was about to vomit. "It appears so, Ryan. He was dismembered postmortem and part of him and the cows has been... cooked."

I almost gagged.

"Nobody had seen John Rook for several days; he could've been dead for quite a while. We'll have to wait for the coroner's official..."

Below the footage a news update flashed: local farmer found dead, his livestock mutilated.

It had to be the dahaka. How horrible. It killed the farmer, cooked him, and fed him to its dogs. I had to stop it.

Sean pulled out his phone and typed in it. "It's less than ten miles north of here."

"What are you thinking?"

"Let's say I'm the dahaka. I have a pack of stalkers on my hands and I have to feed them, but I don't want to be found. Stalkers would likely require a lot of meat. They're large and carnivorous. So I find this farm with a herd of cattle. It's remote enough for me to hide for days. I kill the farmer, start slaughtering his cows, and use the stalkers to patrol the boundaries of my territory and make sure nobody is coming. Except if the stalkers are like dogs, then they'll get bored and start to roam farther and farther until they find something interesting."

"Like our subdivision."

"Exactly."

On the screen a shot of the butchered herd flashed again. It made me sick to my stomach. "Forty-two cows. That's a huge amount of meat."

"I found a leaked photo." Sean showed me his phone. On it a bloody carcass of a cow lay on the grass. Its head, back, and legs were intact, but its stomach was missing, and the entire front of the body was a mess of shredded red tissue.

"They went for the soft parts. Wasteful. This tells me that either he doesn't have great control of them or he doesn't care."

"Either way, he has to find an alternative food supply." I knew exactly where that supply was. Either he would hit more farms or he would come south, toward us.

Toward a subdivision filled with families.

I took a deep breath and plastered on a smile. We had to go out and chat with Margaret before she decided to come in and investigate what was taking us so long.

I sat at the kitchen table. The werewolf sat across from me. Two perfectly round wooden spheres lay on the table, each about the size of a small kiwi. A complex pattern of dark, crisscrossing spirals wove through the wood. We'd fished them out of the pot once the flesh had fallen off the stalkers' bones. The inn grounds had swallowed both skeletons and the disgusting broth and pots with them. I wouldn't be reusing them.

The trackers waited on the surface of the table, quiet and inert. No magic emissions. No electromagnetic signals. Just two harmless-looking chunks of wood. But when I reached for them with my magic, I felt a spark. It curled deep inside them, vibrant and alive, waiting to be released so it could blossom.

Around us the inn was quiet. Caldenia had gone to bed, having delicately devoured enough meat to satiate three grown men. Outside the windows, a sunset burned down, one of those glorious Texas sunsets when the color grew thick and vivid and long stripes of clouds glowed orange on a nearly purple sky. Beast lay by my feet, gnawing on a bone Sean had given her. Through the day she had upgraded his status from *kill on sight* to *suspicious* to *the man with delicious treats who can't be trusted.* She would take a bone from him, but petting was still out of the question.

Sean regarded the spheres with calm interest. "Can you activate them?"

"Yes."

"Did the trackers turn themselves off because the stalkers died?"

"I don't think so. From the scans, they look simple: turn on, turn off."

"So the dahaka deliberately turned them off."

"Probably."

Sean leaned back. "If I were him, stuck in an unfamiliar place, I would want to know where my dogs were at all times. He turned off the trackers. He's hiding, but not from us. From someone who can track him by whatever signal these things send out."

I thought out loud. "He could be hiding from someone he's hunting."

"Or someone who's hunting him," Sean said.

If someone was hunting a dahaka, that someone would be armed to the teeth, ruthless, and powerful. In other words, someone we would be wise to avoid. Or befriend.

Sean picked up one of the spheres and studied it. "You have to decide how involved you want to be."

"I know." If we left the dahaka to his own devices, he would kill again. I had no doubt of it. He had turned off the trackers for a reason, and he would want them kept off. If we reactivated them, he would stop what he was doing and come directly here to investigate. And not just him, but anyone else who could pick up his signal, predator or prey. "We can ignore him or we can give him a target."

"Agreed." Sean leaned back in his chair.

As long as the dahaka concentrated on the inn, the rest of the people would be somewhat safe. I was better equipped to deal with him than pretty much anyone else in the county. And if I did activate them, it would have to be here. I wasn't quite useless away from the inn's grounds, but I was a great deal weaker.

Activating the trackers on the grounds went against the fundamental principle of keeping an inn. The safety of the guests had to be maintained at all times. If I turned these things on, I would be putting Caldenia at risk. But the dahaka graduated to killing human beings. I was in a position to do something about it. Then again, if I made the inn a target, I would put my neighbors at risk. I would have to make sure to hold his attention here at the inn, where I was at my strongest.

I realized I was looking at the portrait of my parents. I wished so desperately I could ask for advice. I might as well wait for money to rain from the sky. I was alone. Nobody would offer me any guidance. I wasn't even sure guidance would do any good. I knew the appropriate course of action: sit on your hands, guard the inn, and do nothing.

Somebody had answer for the murder of John Rook.

"What happened to them?" Sean asked.

"Mmm?"

He nodded at the portrait.

I missed them so much. Telling him this probably wasn't a good idea, but I was hurting and lonely and I wanted him to understand why. "My parents owned an inn in Georgia. It was very old and very powerful. Most inns top out at four marks. My parents' inn was rated at five. It was a thriving, magical place and I loved living there. But I wanted to go to college. Two months into my first semester, I received a message from my brother. He'd come home after a long trip and he couldn't find the house. I dropped everything and got back. I stood next to my brother and looked at the spot where the inn used to be. The trees, the garden, and the house had vanished. There was just an empty lot with bare dirt."

The lot had been completely stripped of any life. Even the grass had disappeared. I remembered this terrible hollow feeling inside. When I was a child, I went swimming at a friend's house and when we ran to the pool, we saw a dead kitten on the bottom. The kitten was a stray who had climbed the fence, fallen into the pool, panicked, and drowned. Kelly's father had tried so hard to revive the little cat. He tried to clear her mouth and pushed on her chest and even held her upside down while we stood there and cried, but the kitten was dead. Seeing that empty lot had felt like that, awful and final. Something terrible had happened there, something irreversible, and the footprint of it had made my heart speed up. The anxiety, fear, and desperate need to reverse it, to somehow rewind time and undo what happened, had gripped me and wouldn't let go, not even after I had emptied my stomach on the bare patch of dirt that used to be our front lawn.

"Where did it go?" Sean asked.

"Nobody knows."

"Did your parents have any enemies?"

"They were like most people: they had some acquaintances they avoided and some of those acquaintances didn't like them, but nobody I would consider an enemy. After the inn disappeared, my brother and I talked to anyone we knew. We came up empty-handed."

"Did you look for them?"

"I did." I had spent two years looking for them and another year drifting aimlessly, because I didn't know what to do with myself.

"What about your brother?"

"Klaus? He's still out there, looking." Klaus had always been a wanderer and he never gave up. I hadn't given up either. I nodded at the portrait. "My sister had married and moved away, but I don't think my brother will ever stop searching. That's why the inn's rating is so important.

The more marks we earn, the more people will visit. One day this inn will thrive and every guest who passes through these doors will have to look at the portrait of my parents. Eventually one of them will react and then I'll start looking again."

The two trackers waited on the table in front of me.

"What would your parents do?" Sean asked.

"I don't know. I know they would do something. They would never tolerate someone from outside killing people in their neighborhood." I looked up at Sean. "If you're going to bail, now is the time."

"I'm in," he said. "No conditions, no strings attached. He doesn't get to come to my planet and use our bones for dog toys."

I reached over the trackers and passed my hand over them, sparking the tiny flame of magic with my power. The spiral lines on the spheres glowed brick red. I held my breath. The spheres came apart, the sections of wood turning like a Rubik's Cube. The trackers realigned themselves, the spirals arranging themselves into concentric circles, and lay still, emanating a steady pulse of magic.

Sean and I looked at each other.

"I guess that's it," he said.

"Did you expect them to explode?" I had, a little bit.

"It crossed my mind." Sean leaned back. "There's a good chance he'll show up tonight."

"Would you like to spend the night here?"

"I think it would be wise. I promise not to try anything funny. Unless you want me to." The wolf winked at me.

"Let me make this perfectly clear: try something and you'll find yourself tied to a metal table with steel cables even you can't break."

An evil light sparked in his eyes.

"Don't," I warned him.

He raised his hands, palms up. "I'll be an angel."

Ha-ha. Right. "What are your preferences for the room?" He would want something clean and simple. Probably with a touch of country so it felt more like home and less like Spartan barracks. I could put him in the Romantic Bedroom for giggles. The look on his face when he saw the canopy bed would be priceless. I began moving the walls upstairs, shaping the room and bringing the furniture out of storage. I had just the thing in mind...

He shrugged. "I don't need much. A bed. A bathroom would be nice. As long as it's clean."

I glared at him. How to insult an innkeeper in five words or less...

"What?"

"No, it's filthy, but I didn't think rotten food and dead hookers under the bed would bother you." The room was almost done.

"I've slept in worse."

Finished. I rose. "Come with me."

I led him up the stairs to second bedroom on the right and opened the door. A spacious square bedroom stretched in front of us. Very light, knotty alder-wood paneling covered the walls and ceiling, giving an illusion of a rustic log cabin. A large, simple bed with a polished headboard that still managed to pretend it was roughly cut from a random block of wood sat against one wall, supporting a soft mattress with white sheets, a small army of pillows, and a sage-colored bedspread. Two side tables, a dresser, and a bookcase, all matching the headboard in style but clearly not part of the same set, completed the room.

"Nice," Sean said.

"The bathroom is on your right." I nodded.

He walked through into the bathroom, which was almost as large as the bedroom, looked at the garden tub, the shower, and stopped by the small windows.

"That's a huge bathroom," he said.

Bathrooms were my pet peeve. "At least it's clean."

He turned. His eyes narrowed. "We're on the southeast side of the house. I can see the road."

"Yes."

"I've spent a lot of time studying your house from the outside."

"Aha." Where was he heading?

"I know for a fact that there are three arched windows side by side with a small balcony in the place where this bathroom is." Sean pointed to two small, rectangular windows situated one under the other to flood the tub with light.

"If you would like a large arched window so people can view you in all your naked glory while you bathe, that can be arranged."

"Dina," he growled.

"People say that physics has laws," I told him, walking to the bedroom door. "I prefer to view them as a set of flexible guidelines."

Sean followed me out. A flat screen TV slowly materialized on the wall across from the bed. The ceiling spat out a remote and Sean caught it reflexively.

"Thank you for staying, Sean," I told him. "I'm glad you're here. You know where the kitchen is, so if you get hungry in the middle of the night, you're welcome to the food. Please let me know if there is anything else you need."

He opened his mouth, closed it as if he'd changed his mind, and said, "Sure."

I stepped out and closed the door. I needed to take a good long shower and wash all the smoke out of my hair.

Two hours later I was in bed, catching up on my reading and trying to ignore the fact that Sean was three rooms away, when Beast barked. A few seconds later I heard a car roll up and stop by the inn. I checked the window. Two Hummers parked on our street. The doors opened and the vehicles disgorged large men in trench coats.

Hmm. And who might you be?

The last man out leaned into the vehicle and took out something long wrapped in cloth. With my luck, it would be a missile launcher. Prepare to be exploded in three, two, one...

The man straightened, his coat shifting. Long dark hair spilled out.

Not a government agent. Last I checked, neither the FBI nor CIA permitted their operatives to have long flowing locks.

The man handed his burden over to another, pulled a couple more out, and closed the car door. As if obeying some invisible signal, the men stopped and bowed their heads, their hands together, arms bent at the elbow, as if holding their hands in prayer. I squinted. Fingers of their hands together, palms apart, thumbs and pinkies touching and held horizontally. The Holy Pyramid. Got you.

I grabbed my bra and pulled my keeper robe out of the closet. They would want to talk and they were sticklers for formality, and I didn't have time to actually get dressed.

Ten seconds later I went down the hall, dressed in a long gray robe with a cowl, broom in hand. Sean was already out of his room and dressed.

"Who are they?"

"The Holy Cosmic Anocracy. I don't know which House."

"That doesn't tell me anything. And why are you dressed like a monk?"

"I need to get you a primer to read." I went down the stairs. "If we're lucky, it's just men-at-arms. If they have a knight with them, things could get complicated."

"How complicated?" Sean asked.

"Very."

The magic pinged, letting me know someone stood at the edge of my territory. They didn't cross onto the grounds. They just let me know they were there. A good sign.

I reached the door.

"Dina," Sean said. "I need to know what we're dealing with."

"Vampires," I told him. "Please let me do the talking."

CHAPTER EIGHT

I stepped outside and walked along the curving path toward the edge of the lawn, where six vampires waited. Sean followed me. The men-at-arms watched us. All above six feet tall, all with identical square bulges under their trench coats, which made them look like football players with their pads on. Syn-armor. They weren't playing around.

No banners. Odd. Usually they had a banner.

"Protocol ARMED," I murmured. "Maximum threat level."

Behind me things slid as the house prepared for battle.

It'd been a long time since I'd dealt with the Holy Cosmic Anocracy and back then I always had my parents to back me up. Now my backup was an unpredictable werewolf who was prone to making snap judgments and acting on them with maximum force.

The largest vampire stood in front of the others. He was big with broad shoulders, a great wealth of brown and gray hair cascading down his back. A short beard traced his square jaw. Human males tended to bulk up with age. For vampires that process was even more pronounced: they grew more muscular and grizzled. The one looking at me now had to be close to sixty. And because he stood with his back to the streetlight, I couldn't see him clearly.

I sent a pulse of magic into the broom. The top of the handle glowed a gentle blue. The vampire's eyes caught the light and reflected it back, glowing pale red like the irises of a tiger. The blue light of the broom played on his syn-armor, molded to the lines of his powerful chest. I covertly looked for the glyphs glowing with dark red. His rank translated roughly to Knight Sergeant. Bad news.

I stopped about six inches from the boundary of the inn.

Another vampire stepped forward and snapped a tube up, holding it horizontally in his hand at about eye level. A dark red cloth unfurled, almost touching the grass. Ah. Here was the banner.

A predator's head with large fangs and vicious eyes was embroidered in gold on the red fabric. It looked like a cross between a bear and a sabertooth.

"House of Krahr!" the vampire with the banner barked quietly.

"Krahr," the other four vampires exhaled and glared at me.

Usually they roared their house name at the top of their lungs, trying to intimidate... Oh. They were trying to be inconspicuous. I bit my lip to keep from laughing. I'd never had an attempt at intimidation whispered at me before.

"Gertrude Hunt greets the House of Krahr and offers her hospitality to its brave warriors," I said. Protocol was important. It kept everyone civil and limited the disembowelment to a bare minimum.

"House of Krahr greets the innkeeper," the older vampire said. "We wish you no ill will."

"Would you like to come in?" I asked.

"We must regretfully decline," the older vampire said. "I'm Lord Soren, son of Rok, son of Gartena, Baron of Nur Castle."

"Dina Demille, daughter of Gerard and Helen. My lord, why are you wearing trench coats?"

"We must blend in," he said. "This is a covert operation."

Don't laugh, don't laugh, don't laugh… "It's very hot," I said. "Trench coats are a cold-weather garment."

Sean cleared his throat. "Half a dozen big guys in ill-fitting trench coats pouring out of black Hummers into the Texas heat? Are you sure you meant covert and not showy?"

Lord Soren's bushy eyebrows came together. "Is there a warm-weather alternative?"

"Rain ponchos," Sean said. "If it's raining. Otherwise, oversize football jerseys and helmets are your best bet."

"Are you sure you wouldn't like to come in?" I asked.

"No. I'll come straight to the point: we've come for one of your guests."

It's like this then, huh. "My lord, if the House of Krahr feels entitled to threaten the safety of my guests, I'm afraid you simply haven't brought enough manpower."

The vampires snapped up guns, swords, and axes. A quiet buzz announced blood blades being primed. When activated, a blood blade could chop down a wooden telephone pole. I'd seen it happen.

I plunged the broom into the lawn. Blast shutters clanged into place, guns swung into view, and magic churned around me, stirring my robe. Next to me Sean tensed, his eyes predatory, his face hard.

"Wait." Lord Soren raised his arms. "Will you walk with me?"

"As you wish." Walking away didn't diminish my ability to target them.

We strolled along the boundary, he on his side and I on mine.

"We seek the dahaka," he said.

107

"Why?"

"It's a private House matter. A matter of honor. We owe him a blood debt and we always settle our accounts."

The dahaka had killed someone. Someone important. "Is this a mission of revenge?"

"It is a private matter," Lord Soren repeated. "He is a monstrous creature. Produce him and this is over."

"I can't do that." Come on, tell me why you want him.

"I do not wish to resort to violence."

"Lord Soren, you come from a predatory species whose members bring down their victims by biting through their necks. At any given time there are at least five ongoing military conflicts between the Houses of the Holy Anocracy. You come to me wearing syn-armor and I've heard you prime your axe. I would argue that you don't have to *consciously* resort to violence. It's your default response."

Lord Soren stopped and stared at me. "I have five men-at-arms. All seasoned veterans."

"I have my broom, the inn, and the alpha-strain werewolf."

Lord Soren glanced at Sean, who blocked the five vampires, his arms crossed over his chest. "Really?"

"Yes."

Lord Soren's face turned thoughtful. Sean had made a bigger impression than my broom or my house. Obviously they knew more about alpha-strain werewolves than I did.

"If we start something, it will be loud and bloody. We wish to avoid detection, but this isn't our planet. We will crush you and leave."

"You will try."

"Even if you succeed in defending yourself, you will be left to deal with consequences."

He was right. It would be very messy.

"Earth is a neutral ground," I told him. "If you attack me without provocation, the Assembly will revoke your House's access to our services. I'm sure House Krahr is a powerful House with enemies who would take full advantage of your travel delays."

He loomed over me. Didn't like that, did he?

"Nobody has to know you surrendered the dahaka."

I raised my eyebrows. "Are you suggesting I compromise my honor?"

Lord Soren paused. I'd backed him into a corner. Honor wasn't a concept a vampire was comfortable compromising. Especially a knight.

"If you were to revoke his welcome, he would no longer be your guest."

"We do not surrender our guests to the first armed person who comes to the door."

Lord Soren chewed on that for a long minute. "Then we shall set up camp and watch the inn until he leaves."

He wouldn't give me any information. Time to end this. "That would be quite useless, my lord, because he isn't a guest."

"Do not toy with me. We are locked on to his trackers' signals."

"These trackers?"

I pulled the two trackers out of my pocket.

"Explain," Lord Soren growled.

"Don't give orders to her," Sean called.

Werewolf hearing. Much more sensitive than I'd anticipated.

"Explain, *please*," Lord Soren said.

"He's killing Earth's citizens, livestock, and hounds. He killed my neighbors' dogs, so I killed his stalkers in retaliation."

Lord Soren pondered the situation. "You activated the trackers. Why?"

"To draw him near."

"That isn't your way. You are neutral."

"Lord Soren, I run a specialized type of inn, catering to a very specific clientele. I don't handle things the way other innkeepers do. You and your men are welcome to join us and wait until he shows up."

Lord Soren looked at his men, looked at Sean, and back at me. "No. As I said, the House's honor is involved. We will handle it alone."

Anything I could say would be perceived as impugning his honor, and his House's honor, and his men's honor, and the honor of their parents and their parents' parents... "That's your prerogative, my lord."

Lord Soren studied the trackers in my hand. "House of Krahr desires to purchase the trackers from you."

"I would be willing to part with one."

"It will do," he said. "Name your price."

I held my hand over the boundary and dropped one tracker into his palm. "A gesture of good will, my lord. Perhaps next time we meet, we won't open our discussion with threats. I ask only that you do not involve my neighbors in your battle."

He blinked and bowed. "It will be so."

Lord Soren raised his hand with a tracker in it and bared his teeth. His inch-long fangs glistened in the streetlamp's light. The vampire weapons vanished as if by magic and his men-at-arms grinned back at him, their sickle teeth on display.

He turned to Sean. "This is our hunt. Stay out of it."

"Knock yourselves out," Sean said.

I walked over to him and we watched them pile into their Hummers and speed north, up the street.

"Thank you for watching my back," I said.

"No problem. Vampires, huh?"

"Mhm."

"I heard a heartbeat and I saw one of them sweat. They're not undead."

"No, they're a predatory strain of humans. We are situational predators and omnivores. They're carnivores."

"How do they get mistaken for corpses?"

"They have thick skin. They don't blush, their core body temperature is lower than ours, and you saw how pale their lips are. They also tend to put themselves into stasis in coffin-like modules when they know they're going to be stuck on our planet and they'll have to wait for a long time to be picked up. Sometimes they bury these modules because they don't want to be accidentally found."

We started back toward the house.

"That's a long way from a walking corpse," Sean said.

"Myths tend to spiral out of control. Do you howl at the full moon and steal maidens to devour?"

"Depends on the maiden," he said.

Was he flirting with me? Devouring didn't really go with flirting, but his tone of voice did. Was this how werewolves flirted? Hey, baby, if I had to kill any girl and eat her flesh, it would be you...

"They look human." Sean shook his head.

"They're similar to us. Our species are compatible. There have been vampire-human hybrids."

He turned and looked at me.

"There are werewolf-human hybrids." I shrugged. "The basic set of genes is the same..."

A howl of pain cut through the night. It came from the north.

Sean spun toward the sound. He blurred and suddenly a monster rose in his place. Tall, muscular with enormous shoulders, he was covered with dense, dark gray fur. His big, squarish head, more wolf than human and equipped with colossal jaws, rested on a thick muscular neck. His hands, armed with two-inch-long claws, could enclose my head. He was huge. The werewolves from my memories would be like kids next to him.

Fear gripped me, born of pure instinct. My knees shook.

He snarled, his eyes bright amber. A deep voice came forth. "Stay here."

"Sean!"

"Stay here!"

He dashed across the lawn, impossibly fast, clearing the hedge in a single leap.

Everything in me screamed to go after him. But with violence so close, I had the inn to protect.

I held very still, trying to listen to the night noises. Gloom drowned the subdivision streets.

Come on, Sean. Don't get hurt and get out of there. Someone will call the cops.

If they arrested him, I'd totally bail him out.

A faint scrape came from the right. I turned, scanning the house across the street. It sat with its side to me, facing Camelot Road. I peered at the darkness under its bushes, searching for any hint of movement.

Nothing.

Something watched me from the darkness. I couldn't see it, but it was there. The hair on the back of my neck stood up. The gaze pressed on me, like a razor blade slowly cutting into my nerves.

The broom flowed in my hand, forming two long, sword-like blades, one on the top and one on the bottom.

Show yourself.

Nothing.

At least Beast was locked inside. The last thing I needed was her getting hurt.

Somewhere in the darkness muscles tensed and ligaments stretched as something prepared for a leap. I could almost feel it.

"Don't fire," I whispered. The inn creaked in acknowledgment. The less noise, the better.

In the depths of the subdivision a dog barked.

The darkness stared back at me with invisible evil eyes. My knees shook. Every muscle clenched inside me. This wasn't my first hand-to-hand fight, but except for the stalker, I had never stood against this kind of attack alone. My parents or my siblings had always been with me.

Now wasn't the time to freak out. Whatever I did would work. It had to work. That's why we practiced.

Show yourself.

A stalker shot out of the gloom under the bushes and sprinted across the road so fast it was a blur, then leaped over the hedge. All thoughts dashed out of my head in a terrified stampede. I spun my broom, turning into it, just like in practice.

The stalker flew through the air, hurtling toward me.

The first blade sliced the stalker's chest. His leap carried him forward. My second blade cut across its flank. The stalker crashed to the ground. The inn's roots shot out of the lawn. The long woody tendrils grasped the stalker, holding it still for a second. I spun my spear and sliced its head off. White liquid bubbled from the wound.

A second stalker burst from the left, clearing the hedge. I twisted and cut across its stomach as it was in mid-leap. Pale blood flew and splashed onto the trunk of the nearest oak. The stalker fell to the ground, snarled in an unearthly voice, and charged me. I lunged and drove the blade into its chest. The metal cut through flesh like a knife through a ripe fruit. The stalker gurgled, impaled on my spear but still trying to claw at me.

A third beast charged toward the inn, galloping down the road. I had to get rid of the second one before I could take the third one on.

I shot a pulse of magic down the broom. The blade of the broom split into a dozen spikes. The spike tips burst through the stalker's chest and out of its back, their razor-sharp tips glowing with faint blue.

The stalker gasped and went limp.

I yanked the broom out of its body, retracting the spikes.

The third stalker was almost to me.

A muscular furry body leapt into the road, blocking the stalker's path. Sean. An armored figure hung over his shoulder, slung fireman style.

The stalker charged.

The werewolf swept the creature off its feet and jerked it up, one enormous clawed hand constricting the beast's throat. Sean shook the hundred-pound beast once, a violent sharp motion like cracking a whip. Something snapped. The stalker hung limp. Its head lolled to the side.

He just killed a stalker, one-handed. Okay. Good information to have for the future, especially if I decided to threaten him again.

The sound of an approaching car engine rumbled from the right.

"Sean!"

The werewolf tossed the stalker on my lawn and dashed to the house. I stabbed the stalker's corpse just in case and stepped behind an oak. Sean ducked into the doorway.

Car lights illuminated the night and a lone truck rolled past us and kept going.

Phew. "Secure the bodies."

Pits opened beneath the stalkers as the house pulled them under. I jogged to the door, melting the weapon in my hand back into my broom.

Inside Sean laid the vampire on the table. A brown mane touched with silver spilled over the edge. Lord Soren. Oh no.

"Console," I ordered.

A communication console emerged from the floor like a mushroom on a thin stalk. Blue icons flared on the smooth metal surface.

"What happened?"

"They were ambushed." Sean pulled at the armor. "He hit them hard. One vehicle is completely in chunks of scrap metal, like something froze it and then busted it to pieces. The other was in a ditch."

Something gurgled, whistling, and I realized it was Lord Soren breathing.

Sean tugged the armor again, nearly lifting the prone vampire off the table. "By the time I got there, their vehicles were in the ditch and two stalkers were dragging him off. He's a tough old bastard. He killed two before the others got him. He was the only one I found. Dina, he's bleeding out. How do we get this damn armor off?"

"We can't. It's genetically locked onto him. Unless he becomes conscious or a blood relative shows up, we're stuck. I can heal him, but not with the armor on."

"Can't we cut it off?"

I shook my head, adjusting the settings. "That's why people killed them with stakes. Back when the legends started, they didn't mean little garden stakes, they meant a sharpened four-by-four. If he were a man-at-arms we probably could, but he's a knight. His syn-armor is reinforced."

"So he's just going to die?" Sean stared at me, incredulous, his eyes luminescing.

"Not if I can help it."

He finally noticed the console. "What are you doing?"

"We can't get the armor off, but other vampires can. They got here very quickly, which means either there's a gate somewhere or they have a craft in orbit."

"And since this is an extraction, they didn't plan to stay long," Sean said. "Either way, they would've left someone to guard it."

"Exactly. He should have a House crest on his body. It'll have that panther-bear with teeth."

Sean plucked the crest from the armor and passed it to me. It was about the size of a note card. I slid it into the slot on the console so it stood straight up and touched the exclamation mark on the console. A tiny red light ran along the edge of the crest, circling it.

"Exclamation mark?" Sean asked.

"Universal sign for distress. If there are any members of his House within the vicinity, they will arrive shortly. Until then, keeping him comfortable is the only thing we can do."

A pale pink line appeared on the wall above the table. It moved, drawing peaks and valleys.

"Heartbeat?" Sean guessed.

I nodded. "If it stops, he's dead."

We looked at each other. The pink line gently zigzagged on the wall.

The only thing we could do now was wait.

CHAPTER NINE

The magic tugged on me. Something skimmed the boundary of the inn's grounds. The pulse lingered, stopped, then flared and lingered again. Someone was knocking.

I glanced at the stairway. Sean had gone to the bathroom to wash the blood off because it "smelled loud" and made him easy to track. Lord Soren still lay on the table. I had sealed him in an oxygen tank that pumped in the optimal atmosphere. Vampires preferred twenty-four percent oxygen in their air. The tank was transparent and now he resembled a warped version of Snow White resting in her glass coffin.

The knock persisted. It didn't feel like a vampire come to rescue one of his own. This was insistent and rude with a kind of mindless efficiency.

I pulled the hood of my robe over my head, took my broom, and stepped out.

The night exhaled in my face, bringing with it varied scents: the damp grass, a hint of distant smoke, and something else. Something foreign. A kind of dry, bitter odor. My body balked like a rearing horse. This stink was bad. It was an evil, harsh stench, laced with pheromones and magic, and meeting its source was a terrible idea.

I stopped in the shadow of the oak and concentrated.

The magic swirled around me. The stench came from above.

I looked up.

It sat above me, on top of the streetlamp pole, anchored to it by large clawed feet. Blue-and-green pixelated armor protected its vaguely humanoid body. A helmet of interlocking plates shielded its head, leaving two triangular ears free. It had two legs and two arms and one head, but that's where the resemblance to *Homo sapiens* ended. Its spine was bent, not quite hunched over, but curved enough to permit it to easily drop down on all fours. Even with the curve, the creature was at least seven and a half feet tall. Its neck was thick, its shoulders massive, and its hips protruded at an odd angle, supporting a heavy lizard-like tail. Despite its muscular bulk, the dahaka looked limber, like a monkey. It seemed wrong somehow, so alien that the mind stalled, rustling through the mental Rolodex of familiar animals, trying desperately to come up with some sort of association for it and failing.

The creature stared at me with two glowing purple eyes. There was no pupil, just the electric-violet iris. Looking into its eyes froze me in my tracks. Instantly I knew it was vicious, cruel, and it thought I was prey. My thoughts and my feelings mattered to it not at all. Given a chance, it would hunt me and eat me.

"Target," I said.

The inn clanged, swinging the massive guns within itself to lock onto the creature.

It scuttled down the lamppost, slid down, and leapt onto the sidewalk just outside the inn's boundary. A deep sound, half subdued roar, half snort, issued from its mouth. The hair on the back of my neck rose. My body threatened to lock into a petrified freeze.

I glared at it. I would not be intimidated in my own home.

A small metal plate on its left cheek ignited with deep purple. "Give me the vampire, meat," the dahaka demanded. It sounded just as you would expect. Like it was a demon who'd crawled out of some deep pit.

"No."

"Then you die."

I had to stand my ground. "Come closer and we'll see who dies."

The dahaka raised his head, turning it like a dog listening to some odd noise.

I pulled the magic to me. My knees were shaking under my robe. The air between us vibrated with tension.

The dahaka spun about and dashed across the street and down the road.

Behind me a door banged open. I turned and saw Sean on the porch. He was in his human shape.

A red star sparked above us, plunged down, and exploded thirty feet above the sidewalk, turning into a glowing orb laced with twisted red lightning.

Sean cleared the distance between us in half a second.

The orb pulsed with red and spat out a man, who landed on one knee on the pavement. He wore black armor shot through with carmine. His long hair, a golden ash-blond, spilled over his wide shoulders and onto his breastplate. He held a long spear with the blood-colored banner of House Krahr.

A Marshal. My goodness. He was the military head of his House.

"They like to make an entrance, don't they?" Sean murmured. "Hey, you! You think you managed to wake everyone yet? Maybe you should bang on all the doors or yell fire."

The knight raised his head and straightened.

I stared. If you had to cast Lucifer before he fell, he would look just like that. About thirty, he wasn't just handsome, he was beautiful, but it was beauty with a touch of wicked edge. He had the kind of face that would stop traffic and when the cars finally finished piling up, he would quietly chuckle to himself about it.

"My lady," the vampire said in a deep, resonant voice. "I've come for my uncle. May I have your permission to enter?"

The Marshal looked at me, waiting for an answer. Considering that his uncle was dying inside, there was only one answer I could give him.

"You may enter."

"Thank you, my lady."

"Follow me."

He trailed me down the path. Sean crossed his arms, shook his head, and joined us. I led them to the door. The Marshal thrust his flag into the ground and ducked inside, where his uncle waited under the glass hood. I waved my fingers at the flag. "Hide this."

The flag sank into the ground.

I nodded and went inside. The Marshall stood over his uncle, his face iced over.

"Remove the hood," I murmured to the house.

The glass rose above the body, lifted by a wooden tendril stretching from the wall, rolled off, and melted into the floor.

The vampire leaned over the prone body. His face turned grim. He leaned over the armor, placed his hands palms down on the chest, and pressed. Red light slid under his fingers. Probably scanning his fingerprints or DNA signature.

The armor clicked and the entire suit of armor split open and fell apart. Pieces of breastplate and leg plates fell to the floor. Lord Soren's bloody body lay motionless. A bright red stain marked his left side. If he were human, I'd say it was just under his heart.

A narrow blade slid out of the Marshal's right gauntlet. He sliced the shirt with a quick flick of the blade, revealing a wet hole gaping in Lord Soren's chest. The Marshal's left gauntlet split over the top of his forearm, and a disk of interlocking metal polished to a satin smoothness popped up. He plucked it free and squeezed the sides. Sharp spikes slid from the edge of the disk, pointing down. The Marshal positioned it over the wound and slammed it down into Lord Soren's body. Red glyphs flashed across the disk's surface. The Marshal turned to me.

"I've attached the field first-aid unit. It assessed the injury and will administer the necessary medicines. The wound is serious. I realize that I am intruding, but I humbly request some solitude. I must pray for my uncle."

"Of course."

"Thank you."

I looked at Sean. He sat in the chair by the coffee table. "Sean? Don't you want to come upstairs to your room?"

"I like this chair. It's very comfortable."

Right. He'd decided he would sit here and watch the vampire. "It's not necessary."

"It won't bother me at all," the Marshal said. "In his place I would do the same thing."

I could make Sean move, but adding force, agitation, and possible violence to this situation now would be disrespectful. I sent a small pulse of magic through my staff. "Protocol VIGIL."

The wall next to Lord Soren's body ignited with a soft glow. A vast garden came into focus, a long path winding its way between the flowers and plants one would never find on Earth. The path climbed up the mountain, passing by the waterfalls and colossal trees. A bell rang, melodious, subdued, and a soft, sad melody followed, floating in the air. A procession of figures wearing white robes, their faces hidden by deep hoods, appeared on the path. The draft stirred long blue and black ribbons wrapped around their hands. Each figure held a long pole with a round lantern attached by a chain to its end. The lanterns, perfectly round and frosted, glowed with gentle yellow light.

A female voice began singing in tune with the melody. Other voices joined in, their individual sounds like stems of a single tree, growing fast and winding around the first singer. The air smelled of flowers, bergamot, and lemon. A feeling of deep peace descended on the room as if the tranquility of the garden and the singers wrapped around us, not isolating us from the world, but gently muting its sharpness to a soothing calm. Soft light spilled from the ceiling onto the Marshal, forming a complex circular pattern on the floor.

He turned to me, his eyes opened wide. "The Liturgy for the Wounded Soul. How did you know?"

My parents had sheltered injured vampire knights before. "I'm an innkeeper," I told him.

He took a step forward and bowed. "Thank you."

"You're welcome. May She Who Heals ease his suffering."

"It will be as She wills it."

He turned to Lord Soren's body and knelt in the circle of light, his hair all but glowing.

Sean rolled his eyes, still seated in the chair.

"Are you sure you don't want to rest?" I asked him.

He leaned over, stole a crocheted blanket off the loveseat's back, and spread it over himself. "See? Perfectly comfortable."

"Good night."

"Good night."

I went upstairs. I had an wounded vampire knight, a Marshal of a vampire House praying over him, and an unstable werewolf watching over them in case either of them tried something funny. If only Dad and Mom were here, it would feel just like home.

Chapter Ten

I woke up because the morning sun was shining bright through the gap in my curtains, flooding the bedroom with honey-yellow light. It was so quiet. Usually birds were chirping by my window, but I guess I'd slept too late.

Common sense required that I had to come up with some sort of plan of action regarding the dahaka. I needed information, and I would have to somehow get that information out of the two vampires. I'd read what I could on the House of Krahr. They were a midsized vampire House with a long lineage and a fine tradition of extreme violence in the name of the Holy Anocracy. So far they had yet to contribute either a Hierophant, who served as the religious leader of the Anocracy, or a Warlord, a designated commander-in-chief of the Anocracy's combined military forces, who would lead them if a foreign invasion occurred. However, the knights of Krahr were financially stable, politically adept, respected by their peers and their rivals, and disinclined to suffer any insults.

In other words, they were a traditional House, which meant they would be secretive and suspicious and would take offense if the wind blew the wrong way. I was unlikely to be getting any answers out of them. I would need a crowbar just to learn the Marshal's name.

I looked at the wooden ceiling. Sadly no answers appeared on the planks. I'd gone through several bedroom styles in my life and my parents' inn always obliged. When I was a small child, I had a pretty princess bedroom, complete with a four-poster bed and clouds on the ceiling. When I was around ten, I saw a documentary about a Dale Chihuly glass exhibit and became obsessed with the strange bright shapes. My parents' inn had grown glass tendrils on the ceiling in every color of the rainbow. When the sun hit it in the morning, my room had shimmered like a mermaid's underwater palace in the middle of a magical reef. At thirteen, I wanted my room to be solid black. At sixteen, some of the black turned white for an uncompromising modern look. I had thought it was very adult. Going away to college was the strangest experience of my life, because for the first time my room refused to change depending on my mood.

When I moved to the Gertrude Hunt, I wasn't in a good place. I had been bumming about the universe looking for my parents for about three years and failed. I had told Klaus I wanted to stop looking, but he couldn't. The kids of innkeepers went one of three ways. A few led perfectly ordinary lives, happy to trade the sometimes uncertain environment of the inns for the reassurance of not having to worry about odd things like two ifrits from different hordes having a brawl in the lobby and setting the house on fire. Others became innkeepers, and fewer still became *ad-hal.* But the majority of us left, drawn away from Earth, into the cosmic Beyond. My brother was one of those travelers. There was too much to see and too much to do. He loved me but he wouldn't settle down and play house with me because I missed our parents.

Once I had accumulated a little money, I returned to Earth and went before the Assembly and passed with flying colors. There were only so many spots open for new innkeepers, and a high score was important. Normally a new innkeeper replaced one ready to retire or opened an entirely new inn, but for some unknown reason they had offered me the Gertrude Hunt, an old abandoned inn that had fallen so dormant nobody was sure it could be awakened. It seemed somehow fitting: we were both orphaned and unwanted. I accepted the offer and coaxed the Gertrude Hunt out of hibernation.

When I restructured the inn and created my suite, I wanted comfort and I wanted to feel at home. I was tired of not having a place that was just mine. I'd always had this romantic idea about a mountain lodge lost somewhere in the snowdrifts. I didn't want to completely replicate that, but I came close. Above me, heavy wooden beams crossed the knotty pine boards. The ceiling slanted at an angle, simulating an attic room, the lowest point near the queen-sized bed, the highest at the opposite wall where a tall window flooded the bedroom with light. The walls were a soothing beige, the thick rug by the bed was eggshell, but the same wide planks of knotty pine lined the floor. It wasn't a fancy place, but it was warm, comfortable, and completely mine.

I lay in the comfort of my bed and evaluated my situation. Right now I had three beings in the inn who were neither guests nor staff. Having strangers in the inn was a really bad idea. When a guest was admitted to the inn, both the guest and the innkeeper were bound by the rules of hospitality. The innkeeper promised to protect and shelter the guest, while the guest promised to abide by the inn's rules. Compensation changing hands sealed that deal.

Neither Sean nor the vampires had promised to abide by the rules of the inn. They were in this gray, undefined area, and I liked things to be clear. I couldn't shake the feeling that somehow I was botching this whole thing up. Somehow even my bedroom didn't feel as secure as it had a week ago.

Lying in bed brooding about things wouldn't solve anything. I got up and went to the bathroom to freshen up. I was brushing my teeth when the house creaked. Something was happening downstairs.

I got dressed and went down the staircase. Lord Soren still lay on the table and the Marshal still knelt by him. A circle of thin sage-green stalks sprouted around him, each delicate two-foot-tall stem tipped with a narrow bud.

Sean still sat in his chair. Beast sat on his blanket-covered lap. They were both staring at the vampire with identical freaked-out looks on their very different faces.

Sean saw me, pointed at the vampire, and mouthed, "What the hell?"

I walked over to them. "Has he moved at all?"

"No. Stayed like that the whole night. Are you seeing this?"

I had expected as much. "He's praying and emitting a lot of magic. The inn is responding a little. Nothing to worry about. Under normal circumstances, I would've given them a private space, but we were in a hurry."

When things settled, I would need to allocate an easily accessible room specifically for emergencies. A hospital room wouldn't be a bad idea anyway, once funds were less tight.

Lord Soren took a long shuddering breath. His eyes snapped open. The buds split, opening into flowers, each with five intense blue petals. At the very center, the petals suddenly turned bright purple, forming a thin round border around five stamens tipped with yellow.

The Marshal raised his head and smiled. "Hello, Uncle."

"Arland," Lord Soren said, swallowing, his voice labored.

Arland stood up. "Why didn't you wait for me?"

"Time was short. I was afraid he would leave the planet."

Lord Soren cleared his throat. "I have failed."

"No." Arland shook his head. "You found him."

"Five men." Lord Soren's voice shook. "Five good men."

"It's in the past. You must rest, Uncle. We'll need you. We'll need your strength."

Lord Soren lunged forward and gripped his nephew's arm. "Don't go after him alone. Promise me."

"You have my word." Arland touched the metal disk and gently lowered Lord Soren back onto the table. The big man sighed and closed his eyes. His breathing evened out.

Arland turned to me. "Thank you for your hospitality. I'm afraid I must impose further. I wish to rent a room for myself and my uncle."

Now was my chance to squeeze some information. "You and your uncle pose a significant threat to my guests. I will gladly rent you a room, but I must ask for explanations."

"You're asking me to disclose the confidential business of my House. I can't do that."

"Then I can't rent a room to you."

Arland stared at me. His eyes perfectly matched the flowers from the floor –the same deep, intense blue.

"My lady, you leave me no choice."

"You have a choice," Sean said. "You can walk out of here."

Beast barked once.

Arland raised his eyebrows. "A Shih-Tzu-Chi. What a delightful animal. My sister had one."

He took a step toward her, his hand raised. Beast bared her teeth at him and growled low. Arland decided that lowering his hand was an excellent idea.

"I have to insist on disclosure," I said.

Arland turned to me. "I ask for sanctuary."

The inn creaked around me, waiting. It was an ancient request. It meant a guest was in imminent danger. To turn him down now would be to fly in the face of everything innkeepers stood for. He'd outmaneuvered me.

I raised my head. "Sanctuary granted."

Magic rolled through the inn.

"What does that mean?" Sean asked. "So, what, he can stay here and he doesn't have to tell us what's going on?"

"Yes."

"To hell with that."

"Do you have a problem with me?" Arland asked.

Sean rose. "Yes. I do."

"Are you a guest?"

"What does that have to do with anything?"

Arland nodded. "I thought not. You're neither guest nor staff, therefore your problem is irrelevant."

They glared at each other. The testosterone in the room was getting thicker by the second.

"I'll make it relevant." Sean's voice dropped into a dangerous icy quiet.

"If you attempt to fight on inn grounds, I will restrain both of you," I said.

"I was always a curious child," Arland said. "I took time to educate myself about the folklore of various places."

"And?" Sean asked.

The Marshal's eyes narrowed. "I'm made of neither sticks nor straw."

"What does that mean?"

"It means you should find yourself another house to blow on."

Ha!

Tension sharpened Sean. Suddenly he looked feral. "That's it. Outside. Unless you're going to hide behind Dina."

"Perfect." Arland turned to me. "I apologize for this rude but unavoidable interruption in our conversation. I promise you I will make it as brief as possible."

"Exactly." Sean nodded, his face frightening. "This will only take a minute."

And the vampire and the werewolf went off the rails. "This is stupid."

Sean opened the front door. "After you, Goldilocks."

Arland's eyes turned dark. "With pleasure."

He strode to the door. Sean glanced out and shut the door with a quick jerk. "A cop's walking toward the house."

Magic chimed. I hurried to the door and glanced through the glass on the side. Officer Marais. Of course.

I touched the wall, shooting a quick command into the inn. The table with Lord Soren slid back through the hallway.

"Stay out of sight," I hissed.

"No," Sean said.

"Absolutely not," Arland said.

I didn't have time for this. "He's a cop. What do you think he'll do?"

"I'm not taking any chances," Sean said. "With all the weird shit going on, he might not be a cop."

"This is a valid point," Arland said.

Argh. "You are wearing armor."

"She's right," Sean said. "You should hide, Tinker Bell."

"I'm nearing my limit," Arland growled.

Officer Marais was almost to the door.

"Go down the hallway, first door on the left is the closet. Change into normal clothes and try to act like a human. Sean, help him. Go."

The doorbell rang.

I summoned every ounce of intimidation I could muster and whispered, "Go, or I will drown you both in raw sewage."

They took off down the hallway.

The doorbell rang again. Beast barked, bouncing up and down. I waited another second to make sure they'd disappeared and swung the door open. "Officer Marais. What a lovely surprise."

Officer Marais looked at me, his face devoid of all expression.

"Would you like some coffee?" I asked.

"No."

"Well, I would like some coffee. Please feel free to follow me to the kitchen." I walked into the kitchen, got out a mug, and pushed the button on my Keurig. Gertrude Hunt wasn't a wealthy inn, but I wasn't willing to skimp on coffee. Officer Marais followed me like a stoic shadow.

"Are you sure you wouldn't like a cup?"

"Yes. Ms. Demille, where were you last night between eleven p.m. and three a.m.?"

I sipped my coffee. "Upstairs in my bed."

We squared off like two duelists with rapiers.

"Did you hear anything unusual?" Marais attacked.

"What do you mean by unusual?" I parried.

"Did you hear anything at all?"

"No. I was asleep. Can I ask what this is about?"

"Yes. Your neighbors down the street reported hearing screams followed by a bright flash of red light."

Thank you, Arland. "I didn't hear screams. Was it a man or a woman who was screaming? Did something bad happen?"

"How is it that everyone on the street heard screams and you didn't?"

"I'm a sound sleeper."

We paused to catch a breath. Sean and Arland walked into the kitchen. Arland wore jeans and a white T-shirt. Out of his armor, he looked less enormous. Sean was leaner, his muscles tighter and more defined. Arland was a couple of inches taller, broader in the shoulders and layered with thicker muscle. Sean could pick up a fifty-pound rucksack and run for miles, while Arland was clearly designed to punch holes through solid walls.

"Officer Marais, this is Mr. Arland. He's staying at my Bed and Breakfast. He's a longtime friend of Mr. Evans."

Mr. Evans made a valiant effort not to choke.

"Did you hear anything unusual last night?" Officer Marais asked Sean.

Sean shrugged and plucked the little container of coffee from the holder. "Nope. Did you?"

Arland shook his head. "No."

"Where are you from, Mr. Arland?" Officer Marais asked.

Okay, that was just about enough. I put my cup down. "Officer, may I speak with you for a minute?"

I walked into the foyer before he could say no. Officer Marais followed me.

"Since I've moved here, you have shown up at my door eight times. I obey the laws, I pay my taxes, and I haven't even gotten a parking ticket in my entire time as a driver. Yet if anything at all happens in the neighborhood, you appear at my door. I bet if a meteorite fell somewhere in the subdivision, you would be here asking me if I personally launched it out of my doomsday cannon."

"Ma'am, I need you to calm down."

"I'm perfectly calm. I haven't raised my voice. You can come over here and ask me whatever questions you want, but I draw the line at harassing my guests. You're interfering with my ability to run a business."

"No, I am asking you questions."

"With all due respect, I'm not legally required to answer any of your questions. Why is it you don't like me, Officer Marais? Is it because I'm not from here?"

"It doesn't matter where you're from. You're here now and it's my job to protect you and everyone here. I'm doing my job and I don't appreciate the drama. Something isn't right with you and this property. Strange things happen around it. I don't know what is going on, but I will find out. You could make it easier on yourself by coming clean."

"Sure. This is a magic bed-and-breakfast and the two guys in my kitchen are aliens from outer space."

"Right." Officer Marais turned. "I'll let myself out."

He turned and walked out. It took all my willpower not to make the door slam to help him on his way. That would be petty.

Caldenia descended the staircase behind me. "You let him goad you."

"I know. He aggravates me."

Officer Marais was a problem. Just how big of a problem remained to be seen. He was just doing his job, after all, and he didn't strike me as a man who would manufacture evidence, so it was up to me to be smarter and more discreet and not provide him with anything to further his suspicions.

I followed Caldenia into the kitchen. Arland saw her, set his mug down, stood up, and inclined his head in a pronounced bow. "*Letere Olivione.*"

He called her by her proper title.

"Such a polite boy." Caldenia smiled. "I prefer Her Grace here. One must adhere to local customs after all. House Krahr, correct?"

"Yes, Your Grace." Arland smiled and took a big swallow from his mug.

"I believe I've met your grandfather, the Bloody Butcher of Odar."

"That's correct."

"I remember now. A delightful man, wonderfully dry sense of humor."

Arland blinked. "My grandfather has been called many names in his lifetime. Delightful was not one of them. He remembers you also. You tried to poison him."

Caldenia waved her fingers. "I've tried to poison everyone at one time or another. Don't take it personally."

"Of course not," the vampire said and took another big swig.

Wait. "What's in that cup?"

"It's coffee," Sean said.

"And it's delicious." Arland drank more.

Oh crap. "You gave a vampire coffee?"

"Yes." Sean frowned. "What's the problem? He really likes it. It's his second cup."

"This will be highly amusing." Caldenia sat down.

Arland shook his shoulders as if trying to get rid of an invisible weight resting there.

"My lord, may I please have your cup?" I asked.

Arland passed me his mug. It was empty. Oh no. Maybe his metabolism was strong enough and we would dodge the bullet.

Arland hit me with a brilliant smile, showcasing his fangs. "Have I mentioned how exquisitely beautiful you are?"

No, the bullet hit dead center. I braced myself.

"I have a cousin whose stepbrother married a woman from Earth. He says –"

"My lord, it's not appropriate for you to discuss your cousin's stepbrother's wife."

Arland's eyes widened. "You're right," he said, his voice full of astonishment. "Personal honor. Very important." He swung to the window. "It's so nice out there. You have a lovely planet. And you, Dina, are also lovely. Did I mention that?"

"You did," Sean said.

"My man." Arland stepped over and punched Sean in the arm. "That was some wonderful stuff. We should drink more of it. I've got to get out of here."

"No, you don't," I said. "My lord, you need to lie down."

Arland opened the back door and walked out. I ran to the door. He stopped in the middle of the grassy stretch of lawn and yanked off his T-shirt, presenting us with a view of a muscular back.

"So coffee gets him drunk," Sean said.

"Vampires have a very sensitive metabolism," Caldenia said.

"He just drank an equivalent of an entire bottle of whiskey," I told him.

Arland's jeans followed his T-shirt. He wasn't wearing anything under them.

"Oo," Caldenia said. "What is the saying? Full moon!"

I dragged my hand over my face. Arland tossed the jeans in the air and sprinted through the orchard.

"I've never understood why some guys strip when drunk." Sean grinned.

"It's not funny. I've got a naked drunk vampire running around in my orchard."

Arland zigzagged back and forth among the trees.

Sean pressed his lips together, his expression strained.

"It's not funny!"

Sean leaned against the door and laughed.

"It's your fault. You gave him coffee. Go get him before he leaves the property and Marais grabs him," I growled.

"Yes, ma'am. I'm on it."

He sprinted into the sunshine and made a beeline for Arland.

"I'm so glad you decided to throw the rulebook out the window," Caldenia said. "Living here is getting more exciting by the minute."

Chapter Eleven

"Naked?" Arland raised the wet kitchen towel off his face long enough to give Sean a mortified glance.

"Don't sweat it," Sean said. "Could've happened to anyone."

His tone sounded casual, but Sean was watching Arland the way one would watch a slithering snake: calm, but ready to stomp on it if it chose to move his way.

Arland groaned and put the towel back on his face. Somehow Sean had managed to talk him down and get him back into the kitchen and into his clothes, and moments later the caffeine withdrawal hit with a vengeance. Now the vampire sat in the kitchen, his back against the wall, an ice-cold towel on his face. Tylenol and Ibuprofen were out of the question. I had no idea how vampire metabolism would react to it, and his personal med unit was busy keeping his uncle alive.

A vampire had once described a caffeine headache as the worst pain she had endured, even counting childbirth. So far Arland was doing his best to be heroically stoic about it.

The coffee maker finished purring. I took the cup, added a teaspoon of sugar, crouched by Arland, and lifted the corner of the towel. He looked at me. "What is this?"

"Peppermint tea. It will help with the headache. No side effects, I promise."

He took the cup from my hands. "Thank you. While I was… drunk, did I happen to mention my cousin?"

"Several times," Sean said.

Arland groaned. "My apologies."

"It's not a big deal," I told him.

"Did I say anything else?"

"What, about a blood debt, killing the dahaka, and how your House honor was involved?" Sean asked. "Nope, didn't mention it."

Arland dragged his hand across his face.

"You don't have to be an ass about it," I said.

Sean shrugged. "How am I an ass? I live here. This is my neighborhood. I'm protecting it and I'm protecting you." His voice slid into a calm, methodical tone. "Let's review: first, this guy's uncle shows up, threatens you, ignores your warning, goes out to hunt dahaka, gets his people killed, and nearly dies. I rescue him, you keep him alive, and then Prince Rapunzel appears in a flash of red lightning, forces you to protect him, putting you and the entire neighborhood at risk, and explains nothing."

Those were the facts, yes.

Sean kept going. "The dahaka is here because of the vampires. They're obviously trying to capture it or kill it, and so far they've screwed this up royally in every way possible. The least your guest can do is to explain why. For all we know, the vampires could've triggered this entire situation. Maybe they bombed the dahaka's planet into the Stone Age or killed his sensei or whatever, and now he's looking for justified revenge while you're wiping sweat off Arland's brow and fetching him tea."

Arland stood up. It was an instant movement. One second he was sitting on the floor, and the next he was on his feet, shoulders squared, fangs bared. "So you gave me coffee to get me to talk."

Sean faced him. "No, I didn't. I gave you coffee because I thought you were a grown-up who could handle a grown-up drink."

"Did you know what effect it would have?"

"I didn't know vampires existed until your uncle showed up here, snarling and puffing out his chest."

"My uncle is a veteran of seven wars, father to two knights, and a man of honor," Arland squeezed through his teeth. "You're not fit to step on his shadow."

Sean crossed his arms. "I don't care who your uncle is or what he's done. So far I'm not impressed. The sooner your armored fun brigade gets off our planet and out of our hair, the better."

"Your planet. Funny, when I looked at it from space, I didn't see your name on it." Arland leaned forward. "Your planet is a trail of dead rocks in the empty blackness. You have no sense of home, House, or honor. You're an outcast."

"Enough," I said. If I didn't stop this now, in a minute they'd be rolling around my kitchen punching each other.

"I was born here." Sean pointed to the ground. "On this planet. This is my home. I don't know where you're from, but if you have trouble finding your way back, I can help you with that."

"You're trying to impress the girl," Arland said. "I understand, but you will fail. Don't trouble yourself —I will take care of my House's debt. Had I known that a mangy dog would get in my way, I would've made sure to mark higher on the apple trees."

Apparently Sean's creative urinating hadn't gone unnoticed. It didn't surprise me —vampires were a predatory species and all the senses that helped them track prey were highly developed.

Sean bared his teeth. The violence shivered in his eyes, ready to be unleashed.

"Enough!" I set the broom on the floor, sending a magic ripple through the inn. The house rocked.

The vampire and the werewolf shut up.

"I will *not* have fighting in my inn." I turned to Arland. "My lord, your room is down the hall. Withdraw."

He opened his mouth.

"Withdraw or I will revoke your welcome, sanctuary or not."

Arland turned and walked away stiffly, the cup of peppermint tea still in his hand.

I turned to Sean.

The werewolf shook his head. "You know what, I'm done. I'll show myself out."

He spun on his heel and strode out.

I shrugged my shoulders. Every innkeeper faced this, most sooner rather than later. When you play host to guests from across the universe, personalities clashed, and if you weren't careful, they would run rampant all over you. Being an innkeeper meant walking a fine line between courtesy and tyranny.

But Sean was right. Arland and his House had put all of us at risk and it wasn't clear why. The fact that they weren't forthcoming with information was hardly surprising, but it didn't make my life any easier. Most innkeepers in my position would've left his uncle to die on the street. We didn't get involved unless something directly threatened the inn itself.

Sean had even less obligation to get involved than I did. He had coped with shocking information well –even if it made him grumpy –but he kept trying to get a grip on the situation by taking charge, and it kept sliding through his fingers. I sympathized, but last time I checked I didn't answer to werewolves. Or to vampires.

Speaking of vampires... I opened my fridge. Vampires required a specific diet, rich in fresh meat but also rich in fresh herbs. Dried wouldn't work. I would need the real thing: fresh parsley, dill, basil, and especially mint. Mints –peppermint, spearmint, and other members of *Mentha* genus –had an almost miraculous effect on vampires. They boosted their immune system and shortened recovery from injuries, and Lord Soren would need some in his diet as soon as he recovered enough to eat.

Parsley and dill weren't a problem. I grew my own under the trees in the orchard. But basil and mint I would have to purchase. We were sadly out of Mello Yello, which kept Caldenia happy and content, and I had my hands full as it was without her getting snippy. Beast was nearing the bottom of her food bucket, and I could use a resupply on a few perishables, like coffee creamer. I took a jug of milk from the shelf, popped the top, and sniffed it. Ew. And milk.

It was almost ten. The sun shone bright. If I had to make an excursion to the store, now would be the perfect time. If Hollywood's best special-effects artists caught a glimpse of the dahaka and his stalkers, they would suffer a collective apoplexy from sheer envy. There was no way for him to travel out in broad daylight. It was now or never.

I took the car keys from the drawer and grabbed my purse. "I'm going to Costco. I'll be back soon. If Sean comes back, don't let him in. If the vampires try to leave, don't prevent them from going but do warn them that it's unsafe."

The house creaked in acknowledgment. I stepped out, made show of locking the front door in case Officer Marais skulked about, and headed to my car.

※ ※ ※

There was something almost serene about walking through Costco in the morning. The clean expanse of the floor just rolled on and on, interrupted only by twenty-foot-tall shelves and stacks of merchandise arranged in neat bright islands in the gray sea of concrete.

Maybe it was the feeling of plenty. Everything was super-sized. Things came in huge boxes and volume was measured in pints, not ounces. It was a false but pleasant feeling of buying a lot at once and getting it at a good price. I could buy ten enormous jars of peanut butter and stuff it in the back of my car. My home was a battleground between a surly werewolf and an arrogant vampire, and a murderous alien was trying to kill us, but I would never run out of peanut butter again and I would get it for a steal, too.

My phone buzzed in my pocket. I checked it. Sean. How had he even gotten my number?

I let it buzz. He didn't leave a voice mail. It wasn't urgent then.

I pushed my cart forward past the tables filled with stacks of clothes, toward the corner of the store where giant packs of paper towels and toilet paper waited. This early, the warehouse was practically empty. Here and there a mother pushed a cart with a toddler in tow. A retired couple debated which huge can of coffee to buy. A regular morning in an ordinary store, quiet. Just how I liked it. Nice and calm.

Unfortunately, walking through a nice and calm store pretty much by myself also tended to clear one's head. My head got itself cleared fast and I ran straight into a hard thought. One way or another, I had to get rid of the dahaka. I had zero ideas about how to do it.

No matter how I turned it around, Arland was my best bet. He had all the answers. However, the rules of hospitality dictated that I treat him as a guest. He'd asked for sanctuary, and I'd granted it. Our verbal contract was binding and could be broken only under very specific circumstances. The grant of sanctuary could be revoked if a guest had lied about the severity of his situation, if his presence inside the inn posed a risk to other guests beyond the innkeeper's ability to counteract, or if the guest willingly and knowingly aided in breaking the concealment provision.

Arland hadn't lied about the severity of his situation. His uncle was truly near death and both of them were in clear and immediate danger. The second clause was usually invoked when a guest was a violent maniac who attempted to attack other guests within the inn. Not only did Arland not fit that description, but invoking this clause almost always resulted in having your inn marked down. It was an admission of failure on the innkeeper's part. If an innkeeper knew she couldn't handle a violent guest, she shouldn't have let him in. Once she did, she had to contain the guest or she had no business running the inn in the first place. It was like holding a sign that said "Hi, over here, I'm incompetent." I reminded myself that Gertrude Hunt could not afford to lose a mark.

The last clause had to do with a guest who deliberately and knowingly compromised the secrecy surrounding the inns. Every planet and every world whose citizens sought refuge at the inns had sworn to conceal their existence and that of the innkeepers. Our planet at large wasn't ready for the big reveal of the universe. People had tried to test the waters –in October of 1938, for example –and the results weren't positive. However, Arland showed no inclination to approach random strangers on the street, declare that he was a vampire from a distant corner of the galaxy, and offer to let them touch his fangs. Back to square one.

I took some paper towels and stuffed them on the lower shelf of my cart. Maybe on my way out I'd treat myself to a slushy. Not that it would help me find my way out of this mess, but it would make me feel better.

I rounded the shelf. Sometime soon I'd need to make an excursion to a home-improvement store and buy some lumber, paint, and PVC. If the inn was going to expand, I'd need to help out by providing some raw materials. Gertrude Hunt had the advantage of age –the inn had really deep roots, but it had stood abandoned for so long. Even though the flurry of recent activity wasn't really straining it, I'd rather be safe than sorry...

A plump, dark-haired woman ahead of me stopped dead in her tracks and I almost ran my cart into her.

"Excuse me." I smiled.

She glanced at me, her eyes wide. "Did you see that?"

"I'm sorry, see what?"

"Over there." The woman pointed to the seven-foot-tall freezers.

I studied the units. Bright square packages of frozen pizza, bags of corn, peas, and Normandy mix. Nothing out of the ordinary.

"I guess I'm just going crazy." The woman frowned.

"What do you think you saw?"

A harsh, grating noise cut through the quiet. Something sharp was scratching across metal. I looked up. Above the freezer on the white wall sat a stalker, fastened to the drywall by its huge claws.

The woman gasped.

Son of a bitch. Out in broad daylight.

No broom. Security cameras. A carnivorous alien monster in a warehouse full of unsuspecting people. I took a split-second inventory of the shelves in front of me and my cart. Shelves: paper towels, paper plates, napkins. Cart: ten three-liter bottles of Mello Yello, big bag of dog food, plastic bags filled with bunches of mint and basil, cookies, twin jugs of Clorox, olive oil...

The stalker swiveled its head, its evil, vicious eyes measuring the distance between it and us.

"What the hell is that?" the woman whispered.

The stalker turned, twisting its body as if it were boneless.

"Run," I barked and grabbed the metal shelves, sending a precision pulse through the building. The magic zapped through the shelving and into the floor.

God, this place was huge. I pushed harder, the magic streaming from me, dashing through the wires under the floor and in the walls.

"What?" The woman gaped at me.

The stalker's muscles bunched.

"Run!"

The woman planted herself. "Like hell! This place is full of old people and kids."

The one time I get caught in the open and my bystander wants to stand her ground instead of running away.

The magic "clicked," wrapping around the right set of wires. The security cameras died.

The stalker leaped, claws poised for the kill. I yanked the gallon-sized jug of bleach from the cart and swung it like a bat. The jar connected with a solid thud, knocking the stalker aside. It flew, righted itself like a cat, and landed in the aisle, sliding back. Claws scraped the concrete.

The beast charged me. I swung the bleach again. The stalker dodged left. The dark-haired woman grabbed a six-pack of Del Monte canned corn from her cart and hurled it at the creature. The blow took it on the shoulder. The stalker stumbled and shied toward me. I smashed the bleach over its head. The stalker jerked back and raked the bottle with its claws –the plastic held.

A huge jar of tomato paste crashed into the beast's side. The stalker snapped at the woman, lashing with its claws. The tips of its talons cut across the woman's forearm, and she cried out. I grabbed a bottle of olive oil from her cart and brought it down like a hammer. The stalker leaped back. I threw the bottle at it.

The stalker made an eerie, whispery growl that raised every hair on my body. The woman swiped cans from her cart and threw them one after the other. The stalker retreated under the barrage of cans, baring ugly red teeth. Step, another step. The shelves loomed behind it.

The stalker leaped straight up, scuttled over the plastic-wrapped inventory on the shelves so fast it was a blur, and leaped straight at me. I had no time to react. The huge claws caught my arms, ripping through the fabric. Pain lanced my shoulders. The impact knocked me back and my spine hit the metal shelves. The red teeth snapped an inch from my face. Fetid, sour breath washed over me.

I twisted the cap off the bleach and dumped it over the ugly face.

The stalker's scream was like nails on a chalkboard.

The woman took a running start and smashed her cart into it, knocking it off me and driving the cart and the creature into the shelves. The stalker squirmed, pinned between the metal framework and the cart.

I pushed from the shelves. It liked bleach, I would give it bleach. I ran and dumped the bottle on the beast's face. The chlorine drowned its eyes and mouth.

The stalker convulsed. The cart went flying, cans and meat scattering on the concrete. The creature thrashed about, spasming, its limbs twisted. Cramps wracked its body. It jerked off the floor and crashed back like a fish out of water, and its head hit the concrete with a wet crunching sound. Cracks split its skull, seeping white slime. It hammered its head against the floor, leaving wet puddles.

The beast arched its back, clawed at the air, then stopped moving.

The woman picked up a set of cans wrapped in plastic off the floor. Ten jars of Bush's Best Baked Beans rose above her head and came down on top of the stalker's skull with a solid, crunchy thud. Score one for *Homo sapiens.*

The woman stared at the ruined body. Blood dripped from her arm. A fine spray of red covered her face –must've been cast off when she slammed down the cans. She wiped her face with her left forearm and kicked the stalker's corpse with her sneakered foot. "Don't mess with Texas."

I looked at her.

She shrugged. "Seemed like the right thing to say."

I had a dead stalker in the middle of Costco. There was no place to hide it. Even if I managed to miraculously stuff it somehow behind some paper plates, it would stink and be found, not to mention I had an eyewitness who probably wouldn't change her story and if someone suggested she was crazy would likely hit them with a thirty-six-ounce can of vegetables.

We were on the verge of complete exposure. Ice slid down my spine. Thoughts came in a panicked stampede, stumbling one over the other. They would come for the body, take tissue samples, snap pictures, and document it. It would be on the Internet within minutes. Once the body left Costco, there would be no way to contain it, and I would be irreversibly tied to it. I had fried the cameras and the hard drive, but my fingerprints were all over the place. The woman would identify me. I had blood and alien slime on my clothes. I had to take care of it here and now.

I had to hide the body.

Now.

"What the hell is this thing?"

"I have no idea, but you need to take care of that arm." I struggled to keep the shaking out of my voice. "It doesn't look sanitary."

"Isn't that the truth. It got you too. You think I should get the manager?" She looked at me.

I gripped the jug of bleach so tight it hurt. "Cleanup on aisle five." I smiled.

She giggled. I giggled back. It came out a little crazy. I sounded like a lunatic who just saw the full moon. I swallowed the giggle. "You go get the manager. I'll watch this, whatever this is."

"Okay. I'll be right back."

"Wait!"

She turned.

"Quietly," I said. "Old people and children."

She nodded and took off.

I sprinted to the corpse and dropped the bleach bottle onto the stalker.

It lay on a solid concrete slab. In a building that wasn't an inn.

Don't think about it. Just don't think about. Just because everyone says it can't be done doesn't mean jack.

The olive oil. I turned on my foot, ran down the aisle, grabbed the bottle, and dropped it onto the body. Cans dotted the aisle. I had to pick them up.

No time.

I crouched by the body, pressed my palms into the floor and concentrated. Why couldn't it have been wood? I could've wrenched individual boards up.

The magic streamed from me, pooling in the concrete like an invisible puddle.

Innkeepers had limits. Basic poltergeist was all most could hope for with a non-inn building. If you could mess with wires, you were way ahead of the pack.

Don't think about it. It's only impossible because nobody has done it before. I had no choice. I had to do it.

My skin went numb, but the inside of my arms hurt as if someone had hooked my veins and slowly began pulling them out of my body.

God, it hurt.

Don't think about it.

Just do it.

My body shook from the strain. The pain wrapped around my spine. I could barely breathe. It wasn't just pain, it was Pain with a capital P, the kind of agony that blocked out everything else.

The concrete was saturated. I could give no more.

I strained.

The pain lashed out like a white-hot whip across my back. A hair-thin crack slid across the aisle. The floor split.

That's right. That's exactly it.

The gap widened. The olive-oil bottle slid into it.

Just a little more. I clenched my teeth and pulled the inert concrete apart.

The body toppled into it.

Yes.

The world was growing dim. I wasn't passing out. I was just stuck in this horrible place between life and dying and it was made of hurt. I paused above the gap and for a second I thought I'd fall into it too.

Opening it wasn't enough. I had to close it. I pulled the concrete back. Come on. I might have as well have tried to push a semi out of the way. Come on.

My legs and arms shook. Slowly the concrete moved, inch by tiny inch. Come on.

I couldn't do it. I couldn't close it.

Yes, I could. It was my duty to close it. I would close it.

The pain wrapped around me like a scorching blanket.

The last inch of the gap disappeared. The concrete smoothed.

I couldn't get up. Oh no.

I grabbed the metal shelving, clung to it and pulled myself up. My head swam. I leaned onto my cart and pushed it. Got to go. Got to get out of the store. I forced myself to walk. My shoes must've sprouted needles, because walking hurt.

I turned behind the freezers and kept going. Through the gap I saw the dark-haired woman hurry across the floor, followed by a man in a black polo shirt and khakis. *I'm sorry. You helped me, and because of me they will think you're crazy.* If I ever had a chance, I would repay the favor.

I passed another aisle, wiped the handle of my cart with my shirt, and walked away from it. My shoulders were bleeding. I veered toward the tables with clothes and grabbed a dark sweatshirt. Slipping it on hurt. I kept the tag in plain view and headed for the checkout.

The shortest line had four people in it.

"Ma'am, I can help you over here!" A man. Average size. Dark hair. Costco tag.

I followed him and showed him the tag.

"Just the sweatshirt?" he asked.

I forced the word out of my mouth. "Yes."

"Your card."

I reached into my purse, fumbled with my wallet, pulled out the Costco card, scanned it, handed him a twenty, got a dollar in change, and then there was the door and I walked through it and out into the sun, car keys in hand.

My silver Chevy HHR was all the way at the end of the lane. I had always parked at the far end of the parking lot, both because it made leaving easier and because it put my car as far away from the security cameras as I could get. Today my habit would cost me.

The asphalt stretched in front of me. I put one foot in front of the other. The parking lot was doing a jig and it was making me dizzy. The heat of Texas summer assaulted me. I pulled the sweatshirt off.

If I passed out in the parking lot, it wouldn't be good. It would be very terrible.

I swayed and managed the last couple of feet, squeezing the remote of the car keys. The doors clicked and I slid into the back seat, shut the door, and lay flat.

Is this what dying felt like? Had I managed to kill myself? Mom? Dad? Do you know what happens now?

Snap out of it. I pulled my phone out of my jeans and fumbled with the icons. Last call. Sean.

"Hello," Sean's voice said into my ear.

I struggled to say something but I had no voice.

"Dina, are you okay?"

What happened to my voice?

"Are you hurt?"

...

"Where are you?"

I tried to hit the button for text message. Someone had turned my fingers into limp things that refused to obey. Here it is. C... O... S... The text showed complete gibberish. Ok, this won't work.

Attach picture. Attach. I got it on the third try and held the phone straight up. The camera clicked. I pushed Send on the screen.

The phone slipped out of my fingers.

If I died in the parking lot of Costco, I would be very unhappy in my afterlife.

Chapter Twelve

I didn't lose consciousness. I thought I would, but I just lay there on the seat, gulping the air like a fish out of water and hurting. My mouth had gone dry and bitter. I had this absurd feeling my tongue had shriveled up and dried out like a dead leaf. Every breath took forever.

This was really, really stupid. If I survived, I would never do it again. Well, at least not without a lot of practice first. Very careful practice, the kind that wouldn't hurt like this.

I really didn't want to die. Thinking about dying stabbed at me. Suddenly I was so unbearably sad I would've cried if I could have. I didn't want to die. I wanted to live. There was so much still that I wanted to do and to see. I wanted years. Years to grow the inn, to meet strange guests, to experience the small, happy comforts. Years to fall in love and be happy. Years to search for and find my parents.

Mom... I'm so afraid. I am so, so scared. I wish you were here. I wish you were with me. You always made everything better.

Sean wasn't coming. He probably didn't even know where I was. I had to get myself up. I had to do something.

I tried to move my right arm. It just lay there. I strained. Not even a twitch of my fingers. I was trapped in my own body.

Nobody would find me. I was in the middle of a parking lot in the back seat of a car with tinted windows. It wasn't even noon and the car was already sweltering. The heat pressed on me like a thick, suffocating blanket. Even if I managed to hold on, I'd die of heat stroke before too much longer.

Get up. You're not going to roll over and just die here in the back of your own car. Stop feeling sorry for yourself.

I concentrated on my hand. No response. I was getting weaker.

All I had to do was pick up my phone, dial 911, and speak. Such a small thing. I had never felt so helpless.

Not matter how much I kicked and screamed inside, my body refused to respond. Sweat beaded on my face.

The passenger door swung open. The hot air escaped in a sudden draft and I saw Sean's face. He leaned over me. His eyes widened. His face didn't change expression. It just turned a shade paler. I must've looked like hell.

"Can you speak?"

...

"Hospital?"

"Nnnn..."

"Inn?"

I tried to nod.

"Don't worry. I've got you."

He leaned in, his body over mine, so close I felt the heat of his skin, picked up the car keys off the floor, and disappeared. The door closed.

Don't go.

The driver door opened and Sean dropped into the seat. The motor started and then we were moving.

Ten minutes. That's how long it usually took me to drive to Costco. Fifteen, if I caught red on every streetlight.

I could hold on for fifteen minutes.

I clung to life. The car moved, the shadows of the trees we passed sliding over us in long stripes. A blast of cold air washed over me. He must've turned on the AC. It felt like heaven.

"Don't worry," Sean said. "Passing Redford. Almost there. It'll be okay."

My back went numb. It felt like I was floating…

I felt the precise moment he had crossed the boundary. The shock of magic pulsed through me like a current from a live wire. I gasped.

"Almost there," Sean told me. "Hold on."

My voice worked. "Thank you…"

The car stopped. The door swung open. Sean scooped me up, shifted me in his arms so I leaned against his shoulder, and ran to the inn. The front door opened and he ducked inside.

The inn shuddered. Every wall, every board in the floor, every rafter and beam creaked, popped, and groaned in unison. The sound was deafening. The walls stretched toward us. The entire building curved. Somewhere to the right, Beast yowled in her high-pitched, small-dog voice.

Sean squared his shoulders, trying to shield me.

"It's okay," I whispered. "It's just scared. Put me down."

Slowly, his gaze still on the ceiling, he lowered me to the floor. My back made contact with the wood. A warm, soothing feeling flooded me. Years ago when my family had gone to the Keys, I'd lain on a sandy bank during a high tide. The ocean water, so warm it might have been taken from a hot tub, had gently washed, at first under me, then over me, until the rising tide lifted me from the sand and I floated with the setting sun and the newborn moon above me in the sky. That's exactly what it felt like.

"Can I do anything?" Sean asked.

The floor bent. Thick, striated tendrils of polished wood wound about me, lifting me up. Sean took a step back.

"Bring me my broom. Please."

He turned around and grabbed the broom from its spot in the corner. The tendrils wound together, forming a cocoon, sliding and winding about each other, holding me up a foot off the ground. Sean turned, saw the cocoon, and took a step back.

"It's okay," I told him.

Slowly Sean held the broom out to me. A tendril swiped it and thrust it into the cocoon, next to me. The cocoon bent toward him, bringing my face to his face.

"Thank you," I whispered.

For a moment we stayed there with two inches between us, and then the tendrils pulled and carried me quickly across the floor, through the new gap in the wall, deep into the heart of the inn.

I opened my eyes. Around me soothing darkness waited, soft and warm. Faint blue lights floated past me like a swarm of dim electric fireflies on the way to their nest.

The tendrils that held me had formed a pillar anchored to the floor and the ceiling. A warm energy flowed through them, the lifeblood of the inn pulsing like the beating of a giant heart. It lit the tendrils from within with a faint green glow, turning the wood translucent so the grain was only barely visible. The air smelled fresh and clean, the way it would smell deep in the woods on a sunny day.

Another swarm fluttered by. The magic was so thick here you could scoop it with a cup.

I had come here once before when I first arrived. I'd walked deep into the inn –it had been asleep and I'd had to force my way through the walls –and then I had sat down here at the inert tangle of the inn's roots, put my hands on them, and fed it magic until they stirred. Gertrude Hunt had been asleep for years, its stasis so deep it was a kind of death. Bringing it back from deep sleep had taken a long time.

Now the tendrils hugged me, sharing the magic of the inn with me. We had come full circle. I had been lucky. My injuries had come from magic expended too quickly. The inn had given me some of its power. If I had suffered severe physical injuries, my recovery would've taken a lot longer.

"Thank you," I said. "But it's time. I stayed too long."

The tendrils tightened a little more, protective, gentle but firm.

The innkeepers have never officially agreed if the inns could feel or not. We knew they reacted, but whether they loved us or simply served us out of a symbiotic need had never been determined. I had my own opinion on that.

"It's time," I whispered again and petted the roots.

The tendrils pulled apart. I slid down and stepped onto the warm surface. All my clothes were gone and my feet were bare.

Something small lunged from the shadows and licked my foot.

"Hello, Beast."

The tiny dog dashed about me in a frantic circle.

A tendril rose. My robe hung off it. It hovered, waiting, as if hesitant. It was so nice to stay here in the serene darkness. But I had an inn to protect. I slipped my robe on and took my broom.

The darkness parted in front of me, walls and dimensions compressing and spinning in a dizzying rush. Looking at it would be enough to send an entire university's worth of string-theory physicists into fits. Sounds of distant male voices arguing filtered through. Of course. I'd left them alone for a few hours. I took one last look at the heart of the inn behind me, sighed, and stepped through the chaotic mess into the hallway leading to the foyer.

"If Dina dies, I will eat you, dear." Caldenia said it with complete aplomb.

"You may find it very difficult, Your Grace," Arland answered.

"No, she'll find it easy once I'm done with you," Sean said.

Caldenia smiled. "I'm amused you think I'll need help, but very well, you may have him first. I do enjoy my meat properly tenderized. Please try to keep comminuted fractures to a minimum."

"What kind of fractures?" Sean frowned.

"Comminuted. That's when bones splinter into shards and pieces. It's quite difficult to dig them out of my teeth while maintaining decorum."

I touched my hand to the wall and sent out a push to isolate the room.

The front door melted, turning into a wall. The light outside changed slightly, gaining a pale orange tint. The doorway to the kitchen sealed itself. So did the upstairs landing, just out of sight. My body protested against magic expended, but if you're going to punch a vampire, you have to punch him hard. This would be one hell of a shock to the system.

"I have done nothing wro –" Arland started.

The northern wall melted, obeying my will. Arland stopped in mid-word. Sean froze in his tracks. Caldenia rose slowly.

An orange plain rolled outside under the purple sky. The wall had opened on top of a cliff and from this angle the vast expanse of the wastes looked infinite. The sun had set, but the distant west was still on fire with carmine and yellow. The moon, enormous, taking up half the horizon, hung above us to the left in the dark sky, the stars behind it bright and sharp. Under it, pale yellow grass climbed up the harsh flame-colored dunes. Scraggly trees, their twisted branches dry, stood here and there, supporting flat crowns of green needles.

The plain stared at them and exhaled in their face, filling the room with the dry bitter scent of grass and something else. Something animal and feral. It was a wild, nasty scent that slashed across your instincts like a knife and whispered straight into your mind. *"Something big is near. Something hungry and vicious."*

The ground shuddered. A colossal creature strode into view on six gargantuan legs, each big enough to flatten a car. It moved fast, the six legs gripping, the long segmented tail with a heavy barb on the end snapping as it trotted. The dying light played across its purple hide.

Sean opened his mouth and stayed that way for a second. Arland's right hand was opening and clenching, probably looking for the handle of his sword.

The monster paused and suddenly reared, resting its bulk on the base of its tail, towering above the plain like a semi set vertically on the road. Its dinosaurian neck bent, swiveling the wide head right, then left. Six pairs of blood-orange eyes scanned the grass. The beast inhaled, fluttering its nostrils. We must've smelled odd.

The beast's giant maw opened so wide it looked like its head had been cut in two, baring a forest of traffic-cone teeth. The creature roared.

It was a sound most civilized beings would never hear, but if they did, they would remember it forever. They would recognize it even in their sleep, and if they heard it again, they would stop talking and thinking and they would find the nearest dark hole and hide in it.

Both Arland and Sean tensed and looked behind them.

"The exits are gone," Arland said.

"I saw." Sean shrugged his shoulders as if getting ready for a sprint.

I stepped out of the shadows and walked between them. As I stepped into the light of the fading sunset, my robe turned russet, shifting its silhouette slightly to adjust itself to the different world.

"What is this?" Arland asked.

"Kolinda. The inn exists in more than one place. There are doors between worlds and some of them lead here. There are two kinds of keepers on Earth: the innkeepers and the *ad-hal*."

The monster on the plain turned toward us, finally pinpointing the source of the odd smells. I turned my back to it.

"*Ad-hal* is an ancient word that means secret."

"Dina," Sean said, looking over my shoulder.

"All those who enter our world are subject to the treaty ratified by the Cosmic Senate, and treaty's most important provision is that it must remain secret."

The ground shook, sending vibrations through the floor. The monster was galloping toward us.

"Those who lose their inn or the children of the innkeepers who have no inn to keep sometimes become the *ad-hal*," I said. "They serve the Senate here on Earth. When someone actively tries to expose the innkeepers, they come. This happens very rarely, but it does happen. They apprehend the guilty and take them to places like this."

The entire inn shook now. The six-legged beast was climbing the cliff toward us.

"My lady!" Arland took a step forward

"There will be no shuttle," I said. "No dimensional gate, no magic portal. No rescue, no way to call home. There is only you and the wilderness."

I turned slowly, just in time to see the furious eyes and then huge teeth.

A cloud of fetid, hot breath washed over me. I tapped the broom on the floor. The wall reappeared, transparent. The beast snarled, confused, but no sound came through. It clawed the empty air in front of it, but we were beyond its reach. My robe reshaped itself again.

"Today the stalker attacked me in plain daylight in front of witnesses in a crowded store. I did everything I could to contain the exposure and as a result, I almost died. By withholding the information, you and the House Krahr become complicit in that breach."

Arland's eyes narrowed. "So this is a threat?"

"I don't threaten my guests, my lord. I have no need to do so. This is a reality check. If the dahaka keeps attacking, I can't guarantee I can conceal it. Nobody can make that promise, because it doesn't care. If the herd of cattle it slaughtered hadn't looked like they'd been attacked by wild animals, the secret keepers would be here already. If the *ad-hal* come for you, I won't protect you. Not only can't I, but I won't. Your secrets endanger all of us and the safety of my guests is my first priority. If you are discovered, your House will be dishonored and banned from Earth."

I sat down.

"We have a saying here. The ball is in your court. I believe you have a similar expression."

162

"The krahr is eating your horses," Arland said. His face was grim. "If I tell you, what guarantees will I have that this knowledge stays in this room?"

"Who would we share it with?" I asked.

Arland looked at Caldenia. She shrugged. "The inn is my permanent residence, as you may have heard."

The vampire turned to Sean.

"Yes, I'll take it to the evening news, because I always wanted to be seen as a complete madman. I would enjoy being locked up for the rest of my life. And my parents, who are still on the planet and are still alien, would be so proud."

"A simple yes would be sufficient," Arland said.

We all waited. He sat down and opened his mouth. "It started with a wedding."

CHAPTER THIRTEEN

"How amusing." Caldenia arched her eyebrows. "Usually it ends with a wedding."

"Who was getting married?" I asked, turning the wall behind me opaque and opening the exits. I'd made my point and keeping the gateway open was draining the inn's resources.

Arland shrugged his shoulders, settling into his chair. "My second cousin. I was in the middle of it due to my rank, and it was a nightmare. Small things go wrong and normally sensible people become prone to hysterics over it. The issue of flowers alone… When I get married, I fully intend to pass all preparations on to someone else. As long as they tell me where to show up, I couldn't care less about how the ribbons are folded and whether they are the right shade of red."

Arland nodded toward the door to the kitchen. "You opened the doorways. Does this mean you've decided I'm trustworthy?"

"No, I just want a cup of tea." I rose and walked over to the kitchen. "Would anyone like anything?"

They shook their heads. I made myself a cup of Earl Grey and came back to my seat.

"A number of our friends and allies had been invited to the wedding, including House Gron," Arland continued.

"Our Houses had been on peaceful terms for a long time, and three years ago we signed the Pact of Brotherhood."

"Pacts of Brotherhood are rare," I said for Sean's benefit.

"Yes," the vampire confirmed. "Treaties are forged and broken all the time. A Pact of Brotherhood is a binding thing. We swore to the alliance in a Cathedral of Chains and Light. This isn't something that can be dismissed with a casual stab in the back."

"Why would you bind yourself in this manner?" Caldenia asked. "Attachments of this sort tend to drag you down."

Arland sighed. "It's a complicated matter involving trade routes, mutual enemies, and an illegitimate child. I could detail it for you, but suffice to say that an alliance was in our best interests. We are involved in an operation that hinges on a great deal of joint planning. The wedding was meant to under-score our Houses' continued commitment to one another."

"Let me guess," Sean said, his face dark. "Someone was murdered."

"The Band Bearer," Arland said.

"They use armbands and bracelets instead of rings," I told Sean. "The Band Bearer safeguards the bands during the ceremony. It is an honor to be one."

"The Band Bearer was a knight of significant renown and extremely difficult to kill," Arland said. "Someone ambushed and murdered her in a rather gruesome way. We found her on the morning of the wedding. When the Cathedral Gates were opened, the entire wedding party saw her bloody corpse hanging from the ceiling, the sacred chains wrapped around her throat." His eyebrows came together, his face hard. "She was my youngest aunt. Our House was dishonored, our Holy Place desecrated, and the DNA and blood of a member of House Gron was found on her body."

The insult had been monumental. Not only had some-one slipped into the heart of House Krahr territory, but they had murdered a knight at a wedding in a church. The House of Krahr had to deliver swift vengeance or lose their reputation within the Anocracy.

"What did you do?" Caldenia asked.

"We kept the results of the molecular analysis to ourselves or we would've had an immediate bloodbath on our hands. Only a handful of people know. Privately we met with House Gron and they denied all charges. They couldn't explain the presence of the foreign blood on Olinia's body, but I've known Sulindar Gron since we were four. We are the best of friends and brothers-in-arms. He swore his people didn't do this and I'm inclined to believe him."

Caldenia narrowed her eyes. "Why, because of senti-mental childhood attachment?"

"No, because Sulindar is an insidious, conniving bas-tard. It was too obvious for him."

Vampires. "Did you ever find the primary crime scene?" I asked.

Arland shook his head. "No. But my aunt did draw blood from her attacker. He'd used a vaporizer to hide it; however, we found traces of an unfamiliar fluid on her teeth. It took three precious days before we identified it as belonging to the dahaka. Their species is rare and he would have been noticed, so he hadn't come through by normal channels. We don't know how he got in or how he got out."

"The plot thickens," Caldenia said.

"It was an assassination." Arland bared his fangs. "That in itself is weak. What vampire needs to hire an assassin? But more importantly, it was designed to create a rift between Krahr and Gron. You have no idea how long we had worked on that joint offensive. This entire situation is a *hissot.*"

"What does that mean?" Sean asked.

"A knot of poisonous snakes that is epic in its vileness." Frustration vibrated in Arland's voice. "Two seasons of planning, gone. There are fifty thousand Krahr followers demanding the guilty be punished, whoever they are, and about as many Gron cohorts placed on alert because their leadership thinks we are preparing to invade them in retaliation. It isn't enough for the dahaka to die. We must find who hired him. He could be working for our enemies, for some third party, perhaps even for Gron. This is the reason my uncle was injured. He wasn't trying to kill the dahaka. He was trying to capture him."

Sean leaned forward. "I saw what it did to your uncle's men. Trust me, we don't have the resources to hold it."

"Spoken like a sergeant," Arland said.

Sean gave him a flat stare.

"Don't get me wrong, sergeants are the backbone of the army. A good one is worth his weight in gold. But they do not concern themselves with the bigger picture. It's not just about revenge. It's about the stability of two Houses. The dahaka must be taken alive."

Sean crossed his arms.

"By myself, I'm outmatched," Arland said. "However, we share common interests. You want the dahaka gone from your planet and so do I. Together we have a fighting chance."

"We don't have enough people to capture it," Sean said. "This is a simple fact. If you think about it for a moment, you'll come to the same conclusion."

"We could lure it onto the inn grounds."

"It won't work," I said.

"What makes you so sure, my lady?" Arland asked.

"I spoke to it."

The vampire stared at me. I'd seen this precise expression on Sean's face before.

"When was this?" Arland asked quietly.

"When Sean brought Lord Soren in. I felt a disturbance, went outside, and saw it on the lamppost. We had a conversation."

"And you didn't feel the need to tell me?" Arland asked.

"No."

Sean already knew –he'd seen the dahaka running away. But since the vampires hadn't been forthcoming with information, I'd kept it to myself.

Arland opened his mouth, but no words came out. Some sort of monumental struggle seemed to take place. Finally some words emerged. "That was extremely unwise."

"Not telling me your purpose on this planet was even more so."

Sean smiled his handsome-devil smile.

Arland considered it. "Very well. That I deserved."

Sean looked at me. "I've been meaning to ask you, what did it want?"

"Lord Soren."

Sean frowned. "Why?"

"Bonus," Caldenia murmured.

We looked at her. She waved her hand with an elegant flourish. "Ignore me."

"The dahaka struck me as smart and vicious. It holds us in complete contempt –it called me meat. But it didn't attack and none of its stalkers made a serious effort to rush the inn. It knows what I am, and it's very careful not to enter the grounds."

"Could you restrain it if it did?" Arland asked.

"On the grounds, possibly. In the house, definitely. But it's not likely to let itself be lured to the inn."

Arland rocked back and exhaled, venting frustration. "There has to be a way to trap it. With all due respect, you are just an innkeeper, my lady. You have no experience with hunting prey."

Okay, then. Glad we decided to clear that up.

"Perhaps we could flush him out," Arland said.

"Not without attracting attention," Sean said. "Attention is the last thing we need."

"Agreed." The vampire bared his fangs.

They stared at each other, then looked at me.

I shrugged. "I'm not a mighty hunter. I'm just a Southern belle who stays home, bakes cookies, and possibly serves mighty hunters iced tea if they happen to drop by."

Arland blinked.

"You broke it, you fix it," Sean said.

The vampire leaned forward and focused on me. His eyes turned warm, and a charming, self-deprecating smile lit his face.

Wow.

"I didn't choose my words tactfully, my lady. I'm only a man, after all, and a solider, unskilled in the way of polite society. I've dedicated myself to the service of my House. My business is that of blood and slaughter, and I haven't been fortunate enough to be refined by a woman's gentle touch."

Sean coughed into his fist. One of the coughs sounded suspiciously like "bullshit."

"I ask humbly for your forgiveness. I neither deserve nor expect it and therefore appeal only to your compassion. Should I be fortunate enough to be forgiven, I promise to never repeat my transgression."

Unfortunately for Arland, I had encountered a few vampires before. "A vampire of a different House once told me something very similar. He even knelt on one knee while he said it."

"Did you forgive him?" Arland hit me with another smile. Vampire smiles should really be outlawed.

"While I was busy thinking it over, he leapt at me and tried to break my neck with his teeth, so no." I'd been fifteen years old at the time and it was an excellent lesson in vampire manners. Despite their beautiful faces, their religion, their ceremonies, their charm, vampires were predators. If you forgot it even for a second, you risked your life, because they always remembered.

Arland opened his mouth.

"I'm not upset with you, my lord. I just have no ideas on how to trap the dahaka. Or how to kill it."

"May I have some tea?" Caldenia asked.

"Of course." I went in the kitchen and took her favorite mug from the cabinet.

"Would a high-power rifle do it?" Sean asked.

"What sort of rifle?" Arland asked.

"Stealth Recon Scout," Sean said.

"Does it fire a metal projectile?"

"Yes."

"How fast?"

"Fast enough to kill a man from two thousand yards away."

"I don't believe so." Arland grimaced. "The dahaka is likely to have magnetic disrupters in addition to armor, helmet, and an extremely thick skull."

I brought a cup of Lemon Zinger to Caldenia. She accepted it with a nod.

"We could try an armor-piercing round," Sean said.

"If I may." Caldenia stirred her tea. "You're asking the wrong questions."

"And what would be the right question, Your Grace?" Arland asked.

"Have any of you ever hired an assassin?" Caldenia raised her teacup to her lips, holding it with her long fingers. Her nails, manicured and carefully shaped, still resembled claws.

"No," Arland said.

Sean shook his head.

"A messy business. If you do hire one for something sensitive, then you have to have him killed, and then you have to get someone else to kill the killer... It's like dominoes. There is no end to it." Caldenia shrugged. "A good assassin always keeps insurance. Some sort of token, some evidence that will permit him to threaten his employer should he find himself in danger of being eliminated, which aforementioned employer, if he is smart, should definitely attempt."

"It's a Catch-22," Sean said.

"A dilemma," Caldenia said. "Most employers seek to eliminate the assassin after the job is completed, and most assassins, predictably, wish to remain alive. With that in mind, ask yourself why is the dahaka here?"

"I don't follow." Arland frowned.

"Why hasn't he returned to his planet, filled with other dahakas?"

"We don't know if it's a he," I murmured.

"Always assign a gender to an adversary," Caldenia said. "It keeps you from thinking you're dealing with a dumb animal. Why does he remain here on a neutral world, risking discovery, when he could be enjoying the fruits of his labor on his own planet where he is untouchable?"

Good question. "Perhaps he can't go home? Maybe he's banished, but even then, he should be moving on, not hanging around."

Caldenia nodded and glanced at Arland. "Remind me, what happens when a craft enters the atmosphere of your particular planet?"

"The procedure is the same for all six planets in the Holy Anocracy," Arland said. "The orbital defenses challenge the craft, which then transmits a passcode by means of a House crest. As the craft descends into the territory of a particular House, the air defenses challenge it in turn. Again, the crest transmits a passcode. For example, we temporarily permitted members of House Gron to enter our atmosphere for the week it took to attend the wedding festivities."

Oh no. "Can the House crest be duplicated?" I asked.

"No. It's genetically coded to each ranking member of the House and it evolves with the deeds of the bearer. It's a communication unit, an emergency power supply, and many other things. A vampire would never part with…"

Caldenia smiled at her tea.

Arland fell silent. "I'm an idiot."

"The dahaka has a House crest," Sean guessed.

"That's the only way he could have passed through the House air defenses. We thought he was smuggled in, but we couldn't find any record of a ship returning or taking off in the specific window of the murder. Of course, if he had a crest, we wouldn't know. The transmissions from House crests work like a key: they unlock the safe passage, but there is no record of which ones are activated when."

"Seems like a security oversight," Sean said.

"We don't like to be tracked. If the dahaka has a crest, he could've dropped into the wilderness, walked out, killed my aunt, and taken off again."

Muscles flexed along Arland's frame. He looked like a cat about to pounce. His eyes shone with red. "To sink so low as to let an outsider have possession of your crest. It is akin to a violation of the House. Whoever did it had to be desperate."

"That's right," Caldenia said. "You are finally thinking in the right direction."

"He still has it," Arland snarled. "He still has the crest or he couldn't have left the planet."

"If you get ahold of it, would you know who it belongs to?" Sean asked.

"Yes."

Arland flashed his fangs and I felt an urge to move back. Beast snarled under my chair. There it was, the real vampire. An unstoppable, furious killer. That's what made them so good at war. If they didn't fight between themselves so much, they could've conquered their corner of the galaxy a long time ago.

"On Earth when we hire contractors, we pay them half up front," I said. "And half later, when the job is done."

"We have the same practice," Arland said.

"So if he still has the House crest...," I began.

"He's waiting for the owner to come and pick it up," Sean said. "The crest is his insurance. He trades it for the rest of the money and departs. That's why he's hanging around here. He can't go home because the vampires won't follow him there and he wants his money."

"And he can't stay in the Holy Anocracy, because any dahaka sighted would be instantly detained," Arland said. "Whose crest does he have, that is the question. Is it Gron or is it Krahr?"

Caldenia leaned forward, her face suddenly sharp. "Think. Think about your uncle."

Arland's eyes narrowed. "The dahaka wanted to kill him. Why...? It couldn't be a kill of conquest. The dahaka had already bested my uncle and had nothing to prove.

It couldn't be a trophy hunt, because being an assassin requires discipline beyond collecting trophies and nothing was taken from my aunt's body. The dahaka kills for money."

The pieces clicked in my head. I glanced at Caldenia. "Bonus."

She nodded.

Arland paced. "The dahaka would be paid extra for my uncle. Soren was a specific target. If a third party wanted to drive a wedge between Krahr and Gron, they had already succeeded. Why pay extra for my uncle? For the same reason, if Gron was responsible for the murder, killing Soren makes no sense. He is pro-Gron and he stands firmly with me and the leadership of the House, but he isn't the main policy maker. If someone from Gron wanted Soren eliminated for personal reasons, they would've challenged him directly. There is no honor in assassination."

Arland stared into space. I could almost feel his brain straining.

"If Soren is removed, his assets and control of his troops pass to Renadra. She's young and doesn't have the seniority, so under normal circumstances she would likely support whatever decision the leadership of the House makes, but she also adores her father, so if he were killed and Gron were blamed, she would seek retribution. Her maternal grandmother is the Blood Archimandrite of the Crimson Abbey. Before the war between Gron and Krahr could begin, the Pact has to be broken. It takes a dispensation from a high knight of the church to dissolve a Pact of Brotherhood. Renadra's grandmother would qualify. Renadra is the only female grandchild she has and she is very fond of her. She would grant her this favor. The Archimandrite would bless this war."

"Would Gron know this?" Sean asked.

"No." Arland's voice was quiet and vicious. "They wouldn't."

"You know who it is," Caldenia said, her voice confidential, persuasive. "You've avoided the answer because it's painful to contemplate. The person is a relative, a friend. But you've seen the signs, the small things, the whispers of discontent, the wrong expression on someone's face. Let it come to you. You can't prove it, but this isn't about proving it, it's about knowing it."

Arland stared at her. His eyes glowed with pure, intense red, like the eyes of a nightmarish jungle cat staring from the gloom at the intruder into his territory. The hairs on the back of my neck rose.

"The dahaka is expecting to be paid," Arland said. "The traitor won't have his crest, but he can send a code that would make the crest respond. So can I. That's how we find our dead."

Caldenia nodded. "There is hope for you yet, my boy."

"What if I am wrong?"

She shrugged. "Nothing ventured, nothing gained. But do be right."

"It's still only the two of us against him and his stalkers," Sean said.

"Three," I told him.

The vampire and werewolf stared at me with an identical expression on their faces.

"No," Sean said.

"Absolutely not," Arland agreed. "You are at your weakest away from the inn."

"Then don't let him lure you too far from the inn," I said. "You will need me."

"Dina, it will take the two of us to keep him occupied," Sean said quietly. "The stalkers will be swarming us. Arland's wearing armor and I have enhanced regeneration. You have neither. They will key on you and there is not a lot I can do about it."

"I might have something that will help with stalkers," I said. "Depending on how much money I can pool together."

"House Krahr is not without means," Arland said.

"I'll let you know if I exhaust my own."

Arland nodded. "If we are to lure the dahaka, we'll need someplace secluded, away from witnesses and with room to move, but not too far from the inn."

"There's a field behind her orchard." Sean said. "It's secluded and hidden by the trees from all sides."

"Yes, it used to be a horse pasture a long time ago. The fence is gone, but I keep the grass mowed," I said. "How do you know about it?"

"I've mapped your entire property," Sean said. "It's in my territory."

Of course.

Arland rose. "I would like to examine this pasture."

"I'll come with you," Sean said.

Good idea. There was no telling where Arland would end up if left to his own devices.

The vampire headed to the door. Sean stopped by my chair. "I don't want you to get hurt."

"I appreciate your concern."

He frowned. "We need to talk about this. In private."

"I'm going shopping in half an hour or so. You're welcome to join me."

He nodded and went after Arland.

I drank the last of my now-cold tea.

"Going shopping?" Caldenia asked.

"Yes, Your Grace."

"Would you like a few names?"

"No, thank you." I got up. I'd need to put on something more than just a robe for the trip. If I was lucky, this trip would only wipe out my savings and leave my legs and arms intact.

"Dina?"

I turned.

The older woman smiled. "Why are you helping them?"

"Because the safety of the inn and its guests is now in jeopardy."

"And the fact that both of them are heartbreakers has nothing to do with it?"

"They are very nice to look at. But the dahaka threatened me in my own house. That I will not tolerate." The vicious edge in my voice was kind of surprising.

Caldenia laughed quietly.

I went to get dressed. I'd need good boots for this.

CHAPTER FOURTEEN

I was dressed and ready to go when Sean walked through the door of the inn. He saw me and his eyebrows crept up. I wore a dark purple T-shirt, jeans, and heavy boots. I also wore a belt with a large knife on it.

I picked up my robe and slipped it on over my outfit. It would be hot, but there was no help for it. "Where is Arland?"

"Rapunzel decided to walk around in the woods to get 'the feel of the battleground.' He won't leave the grounds and he promises to defend the inn with 'all the strength in his body.' I told him if he gets in trouble, he should try singing prettily so his woodland friends will come to the rescue. I don't think he got it."

"Are you ready to go?" I asked.

"Sure."

I picked up a large gray cloak off the chair and held it out for him. He came over.

"Why?"

"Because when people don't know exactly what weapons you're carrying or where your money is, they're less likely to assault you."

"Should I expect to be assaulted?"

"It's not out of the realm of possibility."

I draped the cloak over his shoulders and fastened it in the front. It hid him neck to toe.

I glanced up and saw him looking back at me with amber eyes. That was a mistake. The eyes caught me, mesmerizing, full of some strange wildness, dangerous but so alluring. It was always there, but usually he kept it half-hidden, especially once the vampires showed up. I had caught glimpses of it, like the flash of a wolf darting between the trees, but now, without warning, the wolf turned and stared back at me with amused interest as if daring me to come for a closer look.

Alarm streaked through me.

I was standing too close.

And I was touching him.

Sean wasn't a tame kind of wolf. I had no business staring into his eyes.

"Where exactly are we going shopping?" he asked quietly. His lips curled slightly.

He knew exactly what he was doing, looking at me like that.

I dropped my hands, stepped back, and smiled. "To Baha-char. Follow me."

I picked up my broom, swiped my backpack off the floor, and went down the hallway. Beast ran ahead of me. Hair-thin cracks glowing with electric blue formed on the shaft, and the broom flowed, shaping itself into a knobby staff. A razor-sharp crescent blade formed at its top with a fist-sized sphere in the middle. I shouldered my backpack, adjusting its weight on my back.

"Let me carry that," Sean said.

"You can't carry it. You're my bodyguard. You might need your hands free."

"It's not a purse. I'm not going to carry it in my hands." He held his hands up. "I'm going to put it on my back."

Judging by his face, it would be easier just to let him have it. He wouldn't settle down until he'd taken it from me.

I passed the bag to him. "Do you have to be difficult about everything?"

"Only about things that matter." He slung the backpack on his shoulder.

"Stay close to me. Please don't wander off. Please don't start fights. If someone assaults you, it's okay to kill them, although if you don't have to use maximum force, I would appreciate it if you didn't. "

The doorway ahead of us swung open. Bright light spilled into the hallway.

"Ready?"

"I was born ready."

I motioned to the door with a sweep of my hand. He stepped through and I followed him into the light.

The heat enveloped me, the dry relentless heat of a savanna in the middle of the dry season. For a moment I could see nothing except the bright sunlight that filled the space, golden yet somehow with a light lavender tint. Then the large, pale yellow tiles that lined the road in front of me came into focus. A moment later and I saw tall buildings rising on both sides of the street. Built with sand-colored stone and decorated with geometric tiles, they stretched toward the sky, fifteen floors high, each equipped with a collection of terraces, balconies, ledges, and bridges decorated with the same geometric tiles and drowning in greenery. Here and there bright burgundy, gold, and turquoise banners flapped in the breeze between odd vines climbing down the walls. We stood in a deserted alley. A hum came from somewhere ahead.

Sean blinked at the sun and glanced at me. "This is real, right?"

I closed the door to the inn and started down the alley. "Keep up, Mr. Wolf."

The alley narrowed, turned, and opened into the street. Sean froze.

A busy thoroughfare the size of a six-lane highway stretched into the distance. The terraced buildings rose high on both sides of it, their textured ledges and balconies filled with plants. Stone bridges spanned the street, dangerously high. Merchant stalls sprouted here and there under bright canvas cloth, offering strange fruits in ornate crates, robotic parts, high-grade cybernetics, perfume, paint, caged creatures, weapons, and jewelry. Open doors under glowing signs invited shoppers, and the merchants waved holographic images of their wares at the crowd in the street.

A mass of creatures moved through it all, colorful, varied, and loud. Some were human, some furry, some feathered, others wrapped in cloth or armor. The air vibrated with hundreds of haggling voices and sounds of boots, hooves, and claws scraping the tiles. The breeze brought the aroma of cooked meat, tart and bitter spices, and the multilayered, complex scents of the crowd.

Above it all in the purple sky, a colossal lavender planet rose, ethereal and pale. Huge chunks of it hung motionless, separated from the main mass, as if the planet had been made of clay and someone had shattered its edge with a precise blow of a hammer.

"What is this?" Sean whispered next to me.

"The Node. This is Baha-char. The place to buy things."

He looked shell-shocked. His nostrils flared. He must've been sorting through all the different scents. I'd been coming to the Node since I was five years old. For me it was exciting but familiar. For him, with all the different noises, smells, and creatures, it was probably overwhelming.

"Come on." I stepped into the traffic. He followed me. We turned right and moved with the flow of the crowd. Beast trotted a few steps ahead of us, clearly in charge of the expedition.

To the left a small hooded creature darted through the crowd. A tall woman, skeletally thin and wrapped in hundreds of silvery chains, chased after it, yelling. The creature zigzagged and veered right. The woman tried to follow and collided with a large cloaked creature. He whirled around, his face an odd meld of dinosaur and human, and lunged at her. The woman howled and raked him with long claws. They ripped into each other, rolling on the ground. The crowd parted around them and kept moving, leaving them snarling and growling.

"Fun place," Sean said.

"Whatever you're looking for, you will find it at Bahachar," I said. "That includes trouble."

We crossed the street and turned left into one of the side streets, which was only slightly less wide. Here the traffic was lighter. To the left and slightly in front of us, two men walked shoulder to shoulder. The first wore leather pants, a white shirt with wide sleeves, and a leather vest over it. A wide leather bracer enclosed his left forearm. His hair, a rare blond shade, almost gold, hung in a ponytail down his back. He moved with a casual aristocratic elegance, perfectly balanced. Watching him, you had a feeling that if the road suddenly became a tightrope, he would just keep on walking without breaking a stride. My father moved like that. I sped up a little. We drew even and I saw a slender sword on his waist. That's what I thought. An expert swordsman.

I glanced at his face and blinked. He was remarkably handsome.

The man to his left was larger, his shoulders broader, his body emanating contained aggression. He didn't walk, he stalked, and you could tell by the way he moved that he would be very strong. His auburn hair looked like he'd rolled out of bed, dragged his hand through it, and gone on about his day. He wore dark pants and a black leather jacket that was more doublet than motorcycle. A ragged scar crossed his left cheek and when he turned his head, his eyes shone with yellow. Interesting.

"It's always work with you," the russet-haired man said.

"Some of us have to mind the safety of the realm," the blond said. A narrow smile curled his lips.

"I've given the realm eight years of my life. It can bite me," his stocky companion retorted. "How far is it?"

The slim man raised his left arm. A hawk dropped out of the sky and landed on his bracer. "We're almost there. Two blocks left."

"Good. Let's get this crap and go home."

They turned into the side street.

"That bird smelled dead," Sean said.

"Dead?"

He nodded. "A couple of days at least. Tell me something. Why live on Earth when you can live here?"

"Some people go to exotic places on vacation and fall in love with them. Some of them even stay and then, once the newness wears off, they find that this new place is just as rough and mundane as the one they left. Other people go to exotic places, visit, and then say 'That's nice, but I miss my house and it's time to go home.' Earth is home. There is no prettier sky, there is no greener grass, and there is no place that feels as right."

He mulled that over.

We made a right, then another right, and stopped before a large building. A rectangular doorway gaped in the middle, dark like the mouth of some beast. A gray-skinned woman blocked it. Her dark hair fell below her waist in thin dreads. She looked at us with gold eyes, saw my face, and smiled, showing a mouth full of sharp, triangular teeth.

"Greetings, Dina."

"Greetings, *saar ah*. Will the Merchant see me?"

"Nuan Cee always has time for you." *Saar ah* stepped aside. "Come on in."

The foyer opened into a large room. Large square tiles, gray with the familiar geometric border, lined the floor and climbed the walls. Green, blue, and dark purple plants grew here and there in ornate pots. At the far wall, a long slit spilled water across tile and it ran down the twenty-foot wall to fall into a narrow basin with a soft splash.

A low table, carved from a solid block of volcanic glass, stood to the left, surrounded by comfortable, dark purple sofas. *Saar ah* led us to it, smiled and showed her shark teeth, then went to stand by the wall. We both remained standing.

"What is she?" Sean asked me quietly.

"I've seen her people a couple of times, but they are reclusive and usually keep to their own world. I can tell you that for *saar ah* to serve a Merchant, she would have to be really good. There are hundreds of vendors at the Baha-char, but only a few dozen of them are Merchants. Merchants handle significant transactions and to become one, you have to have a fleet and show a lot of profit. Some of them specialize in large shipments. Some like Nuan Cee, deal in rare goods. Basically, if you want something you can't readily buy on the street because it's hard to find or you need it in a large quantity, you go to a Merchant."

"Anything I need to know about this particular Merchant?" Sean asked.

"Nuan Cee is vain, fussy, and difficult." I glanced at *saar ah*. "Anything I left out?"

A flash of shark teeth. "Excitable."

"That too. He is also rich and very respected, and if he can't get what you're looking for, then what you're asking for is impossible." Chances were, Nuan Cee was listening to us and a little flattery never hurt.

The gauzy lavender-and-blue curtain on the right parted, and a creature stepped into view. He walked upright but stood barely four feet tall, including the six-inch lynx ears. Short, silver-blue fur covered his frame like soft velvet, dappled with pale golden rosettes on his back and fading to almost white on his stomach. His face would've been feline if it weren't for an elongated muzzle that resembled a fox's snout. He wore a silk apron and jewelry made from small cream and blue shells. His large round eyes were bright with vivid turquoise irises.

He smiled at me, showing sharp teeth. "Dina. Come sit, sit, sit."

We sat.

He glanced at Sean. "I see you have finally employed *Saar ah*."

"He is a friend," I told him. "I don't need a bodyguard. I am not important like the great Nuan Cee."

The Merchant smiled. "I do like to converse with you. You are always most pleasant." His furry face turned somber. "Have you news of your parent figures?"

"No."

He nodded. "I have kept my ear to the wind but there are no answers, only whispers too vague to sense. Should I hear something, I shall send word."

That word would be expensive, but I would pay for it, whatever the price might be.

"So how can this humble trader help you today?"

"I'm looking to purchase a clutch of Anansi pearls."

Nuan Cee leaned forward. His eyes shone with predatory glee. His lips parted, revealing carnivore fangs in a disturbing smile. "Ooooh. You're going to ki…i…ill someone. Who is it? Is it someone I know?"

"Probably not."

He laughed like a cat sneezing and waved his paw-hands. "Very good, very good, keep your secrets, keep, keep. Now then, what have you brought in trade?"

I'd brought a couple of things. My parents had traded with Nuan Cee; I'd watched them make deals since I was a toddler. Things like gold and jewels meant nothing to a rare-goods trader. After all, gold was just a metal that could be found on hundreds of worlds. Nuan Cee wanted something unique and rare. Something wrapped in legend. And to pay for Anansi pearls, that something had to be very special.

Sean passed me the backpack. I unzipped it and pulled out three large bottles. Each had a yellow label with a portrait of an older man smoking a cigar. "Pappy Van Winkle's fifteen-year-old Family Reserve bourbon. Best small-batch bourbon in show at San Francisco's World Spirits. Nearly impossible to get."

As an opening trade, it wasn't half-bad. It had taken me forever to get the bourbon, and I knew for a fact that Nuan Cee kept up with the alcohol trade on dozens of planets. This was my proof that I could procure something rare.

Nuan Cee leaned forward, enthusiastic. "Interesting. Four pearls. Five for you. Your parent figures always brought me the best things, and I will be generous in their memory."

Five wouldn't cut it. He wanted the bourbon, but not nearly enough. It was time for the real thing. Here's hoping it did its job well enough.

I reached into the backpack and extracted a small jar wrapped in bubble wrap. I peeled the wrap off and set the jar on the table. Nuan Cee peered at the viscous yellow fluid within.

"What would this be?"

"A treasure." I leaned forward and moved the jar. The ray of sun from the window pierced the contents and the liquid glowed like molten gold.

Nuan Cee's eyes sparked.

"On Earth, far to the south of me and near the equator, lies a sea, a pure crystalline blue. At its north edge, where two continents touch, stretches an arid plain. As one moves farther from the water, the plain rises and turns into barren hills and desolate mountains. Between the mountains hide wadis, narrow fertile valleys, secreted from the world. It is an ancient land, named after a ruthless warlord. Legend says he was so devastating in battle that his enemies knew facing his army meant the end of their existence. They called this place Hadramout. It means 'death has arrived.'"

Nuan Cee was listening.

"Twice a year, simple artisans make the arduous trek through these mountains as their ancestors have done for seven thousand years. They climb the secret trails to the east, toward the rising sun, until they come to the valley where the sidr trees grow. The sidr are sacred to many religions. Muslims know them as trees of Paradise. Christians believe that when Man was cast from the Garden of Eden by God, it was the fruit of the sidr tree that first gave him sustenance. Its roots dig deep into the soil, so far it can survive the most ferocious floods and droughts. Every part of the tree is medicinal, every leaf is precious. But the artisans take none of it. Carefully, gingerly, they harvest the honey from the bees that feed on the pollen of those trees and make their long perilous journey back. The sidr honey they bring with them cures many ills. It is the essence of that ancient, savage land. It's very lifeblood. There is none rarer or more highly prized."

Nuan Cee looked at the jar. "Twelve."

I rose. "My apologies. I hadn't realized that great Nuan Cee had fallen on hard times. Forgive me. I meant no offense."

Nuan Cee hissed at the insult. I reached for the jar.

"Twenty," he barked.

I pondered the jar in front of me. It felt like walking a tightrope. If the deal fell through, I had no idea where to go next. "I'm in great need. That's the only reason I'm willing to part with it. I bargain for my life, Merchant. You know my price."

"Thirty-two," he said. "The full clutch. It is my final offer."

I waited for the painful five seconds. "We have a deal."

Twenty minutes later we left Nuan Cee's warehouse, pushing a heavy cart in front of us. Inside, in sealed crates, rested the Anansi pearls. Thirty-two. Enough to murder a battalion of Navy SEALs. Maybe two battalions.

"Do Navy SEALs have battalions?" I asked.

"No. SEALs have teams, which are organized into warfare groups. Each team has several platoons in it, usually six. The Army has battalions. Was any of that story true?"

"About the honey? Yes. It's the most expensive honey in the world and it's harvested in Yemen."

He grunted. "How much did it set you back?"

"That jar he has is one kilo, so about two point two pounds. It goes for about ninety dollars a pound. With shipping, it ends up being around two fifty per large jar. Of course, you have to know where to buy the real thing…"

Sean stared at me.

"What?"

"Two hundred and fifty bucks?"

"Well, it's honey, not white truffles. There is a price ceiling there."

"What happens when he realizes you sold him a jar of honey he could've gotten for two hundred and fifty dollars?"

"I sold him the rarest, most expensive honey on planet Earth. Exactly as advertised. He will use my story to resell it for thousands in whatever currency he wishes. If he decides I got the better of him, it will just make him respect me more."

Sean shook his head.

"Besides, if things went sour, you would totally spring to my rescue. I'm sure if you did some ferocious growling…"

Sean stopped and peered down the alley. I listened. A quiet melody floated on the breeze, beautiful and sad. It came from the dark archway just ahead. Sean pushed the cart forward, forgetting I was there, and stopped before the door.

A man leaned against the doorway. Tall, broad-shouldered, with a mane of graying hair, he watched us from the shadows. The light caught his eyes and they flashed with telltale yellow. A werewolf.

Next to me Sean went really still. He wasn't afraid. He just waited, loose and ready, watching, listening.

"What unit?" the man called out.

Sean didn't answer.

"I asked you a question, soldier. Where you stationed?"

"Fort Benning," Sean said. "I didn't fight for your world in your war. I fought for my country in mine."

The man stepped forward. Weather and age had chiseled his face. He looked grizzled, scuffed around the edges like an old gun, but no less deadly. He inhaled deeply.

"Alpha strain. You can't be more than thirty. That would make you Earthborn." He slumped a little against the doorway. "Well, how about that. We achieved viable offspring after all. Come inside. You're my life's work. You have nothing to fear from me."

CHAPTER FIFTEEN

The inside of the shop was neat, its wares arranged under glass, along the counter, and on the walls with military precision. Knives in wooden display stands, curved crescent weapons, metal canisters of unknown purpose, leather harnesses and belts, boots, jewelry, boxes filled with dark orange powder, vials with turquoise liquid... Stepping into this place was like walking into another world.

"Gorvar!" the older werewolf growled.

An enormous blue-green animal padded through the other door. The creature's head, even with massive ears and a thick dark mane, came up to my chest. The lines of its head and the long body said wolf, but the difference between an Earth wolf and this creature was like the difference between a puppy and the leader of a pack. On our world, it would be the king of all wolves.

"Go watch the cart," the werewolf said.

The wolf padded out the door.

The older werewolf took a glass cup filled with small round spheres, each about the size of a walnut, from the counter, plucked one out, and held it between his index finger and thumb. "Know what these are?" he said to Sean.

"No."

"Cluster bombs."

The werewolf gently placed the sphere back in the glass, looked at the cup, and hurled the contents at Sean.

Time stopped.

My chest began to rise as my lungs sucked in air in panic. The shiny glass spheres flew through the air.

Sean moved, a blur slicing through the room like a knife.

Some invisible omnipotent being pressed Play on the remote. I exhaled and blinked. Sean's left hand held the spheres. His right pressed a knife to the older werewolf's throat.

The older man raised his hand slowly and checked his wrist. Blue symbols glowed under his skin.

"Point six seconds. You are the real thing." He grinned, baring white teeth. "The real thing."

"I think you might be crazy," Sean said.

"You have no idea how amazing it is that you're alive. Sorry about the scare. They're not armed. No detonators. I just had to know." The werewolf took a sphere from Sean's hand and tossed it on the ground. It rolled harmlessly on the floorboards. "I sell them as souvenirs. Own a piece of tech from the dead planet. The tools of our own destruction available for twenty credits each to the discerning shopper."

He smiled and took a slow step back. Sean let him go and dropped the knife back onto the counter. I hadn't even seen him pick it up.

The older werewolf crossed the shop, slid open a panel in the wall, and took out a glass pitcher filled with dark purple liquid.

"Go ahead, look around. This is as close as you'll come to Auul. Like it or not, this was the planet that breathed life into your parents. Your heritage."

Sean slid the spheres back into the cup and turned, scanning the surroundings. He looked like a man who'd just found out his much-admired ancestor was a serial killer and was now standing in his tomb, unsure how he felt about it.

"Name is Wilmos Gerwar, 7-7-12," the older werewolf said, adding three ornate glasses to the pitcher. "Seventh Pack, Seventh Wolf, Twelfth Fang. Gerwar stands for Medic."

"No last name?" I asked.

"No. Used to be more complicated than that. Used to be you had a tribe and would list your ancestors for four generations after your name. But when the war started, it was decided that short was best. Besides, it didn't matter much who you were anymore. People died so fast it only mattered what you did. I was the thirty-second Gerwar in my Fang. It was a long war."

Wilmos took the glasses and the pitcher to a small table and invited me to sit. I slid onto the padded bench. Beast curled by my feet. Wilmos filled the glasses and pushed one toward Sean.

"No thanks," Sean said.

Wilmos took a swallow from his glass. "This is Auul tea. I know a former Boom-Boom –that would be heavy-artillery gunner –who owns land in Kentucky. He's got five acres of this stuff. Exports it to a half dozen dealers, what few of us are left in the Galaxy. I wouldn't poison you. And I would never poison an innkeeper." He held the glass out to me. "We all need a refuge once in a while."

I took a sip. The tea tasted tart and refreshing and strangely alien. I couldn't quite put my finger on it, but there was a hint of something not quite Earth-like about the flavor.

Sean took the third chair and tasted the tea. I couldn't tell by his face if he liked it or hated it. His gaze kept going to a spot in the corner. There, under the blue glow of a small force field, lay a suit of armor. Dark gray, almost black, it looked like a chainmail made of small, sharp scales, if chainmail could be thin like silk. On the shoulders, the scales flared into the plates. The faint image of a maned wolf marked the chest, somehow formed by the lines of the interlocking scales. It looked like a suit of armor, but it couldn't possibly be one –it was too thin.

"I'm fourth generation," Wilmos said. "My parents were werewolves and their parents and theirs were also. When I was young, I never thought I'd have to serve. We had beaten Mraar. I was looking toward a peaceful future. I was a nanosurgeon. Then the Raoo of Mraar reconstructed the ossai and made the Sun Horde. Damn cats. Our secret weapon was no longer secret and we knew the end was coming. It would be long and bloody, but it was inevitable. Most people turned to work on the gates. I was working on those who would keep the gates open."

He drained his glass and refilled it. "There were two dozen of us, geneticists, surgeons, medics. We bred the alphas from scratch. Anybody ever call you *probira?*"

"No," Sean said. His gaze darkened. "Maybe. Once."

"Before the war, Mraar's main export was cybernetics. You know what Auul's was? Poets." Wilmos laughed. "We were big on arts and humanities. It was all about family and proper education. Our civilization had produced thousands of books on how to properly rear your offspring so they would become 'beautiful souls.' If a child hadn't composed a heroic saga by age ten, the parents would take him to a specialist to have his head examined. Even in war, we'd win a victory and then spend twice as much energy writing songs about it. Moon-gazing and soul-searching was highly encouraged. When I was a little younger than you, I spent a year alone in the wild. Only took a small backpack with me. I felt like I was too soft and wanted to see if I could be hard. Almost like I needed to punish myself, you understand?

Sean nodded. I guess maybe he did. I'd never had an urge to live in the wilderness by myself, so he was on his own there.

"Your parents were conceived and brought to term in an artificial environment. What's the saying on Earth?" He glanced at me.

"Test-tube babies."

"Yes. That. We'd tried implanting embryos into volunteers, but the new modifications were simply too different. We had reengineered the ossai, and this new, improved alpha ossai conflicted with the ossai already inside the surrogate mothers. When we were lucky, the pregnancy ended in miscarriage. When we weren't, it killed the mother." He paused. "There were those who had serious doubts about the wisdom of growing babies outside the womb. They questioned their... humanity."

Sean's face turned hard. "What does *probira* mean?"

"Soulless," Wilmos said.

Ouch.

Sean nodded. "I thought as much."

So that's why the other werewolves shunned them. Made sense.

"They called us the monster makers. Parents of subhumans. There was a lot of discussion about whether it would be better to perish than to chance releasing something soulless into the universe. But in the end everyone agreed we needed alphas or none of us would make it. For all our grandstanding, we are a selfish lot. Nobody expected the alphas to survive. Or breed. I always had hope."

"Why?" Sean asked.

Wilmos leaned on the table. "I was with your parents' generation until they were five. I watched them smile for the first time. I helped them take their first steps. They were as real and alive as any normal children. A soul, if such a thing exists at all, doesn't filter into you at birth through your mother's umbilical cord. Souls come from the people who shape you as you grow. The alphas were children. My children. And I took care of them the best I could. All of us on the team did and all the while we knew we would be sending them to the slaughter. They would be the last line of defense. Bullet meat."

Wilmos shrugged and smiled. It looked forced. "As I said, we tend to brood. It was a long time ago. We all made sacrifices. You never told me who your parents were."

"You don't need to know that," Sean said.

"Good," Wilmos said. "No need to share secrets if you don't have to. That's a winning strategy. At least tell me what you do. What they do? Were they able to adjust? How did your childhood go?"

"Both of my parents joined the Earth's military," Sean said. "They did well and retired. My father is a lawyer. My mother helps him. They're almost never apart. They like books and violent computer games. They go fishing but don't catch anything. They just sit together with their fishing rods and talk. I didn't understand what they got out of it until much later, after I enlisted and realized it was their off mode. It used to drive me nuts when I was a kid. I thought they were boring. I had a normal childhood, or as normal as you can get being an Army brat and a werewolf. There were a few incidents because of turning, but nothing major. Lots of sports, lots of moving. My parents live simply, but I was a spoiled kid. I had all the cool toys and all the right clothes. I could've gone to college, but instead I enlisted. I didn't feel like I belonged where I was and I wanted to be on my own. Also, I was angry at my parents. Why, I don't even know. For providing me with a comfortable life, I suppose. I was going stir-crazy and felt entitled to some tragedy to be bummed out about, but I didn't have any."

"I know the feeling," Wimos said. He leaned forward, focused on Sean. "How long were you in? Was it hard? Why did you get out? Tell me."

"I did eight years, several small conflicts, and two wars. The Army was easy. Be where you're supposed to be when you're supposed to be there and do as you're told. I was the fastest and the strongest. I killed people, sometimes at close range. I didn't love it, but I didn't lose much sleep over it either. It was a job and I was very good at it. I liked being in. It took the edge off and I felt normal. I got promoted quickly, E-5 in three years, E-6 in five. The Army provides you with a place to sleep, feeds you, outfits you. If you don't have a family and don't care about the latest car with the shiniest rims, there's not much opportunity to spend the money. I put away half my paycheck since day one and once a year I would go to places the Army didn't send me. I've been on six continents out of seven, and the seventh is a frozen wasteland. I kept looking for the place that felt right and none of them ever did. Two years into my E-6, they started pushing me to E-7, Sergeant First Class. It's almost always an admin job. E-6 was as high as I could go and still stay with the soldiers. I knew if they chained me to a desk, I'd go off the cliff."

Sean leaned back and took another swallow of tea. "I fought them on it as long as I could, and when I couldn't anymore, I finished out my time and got out. When I first got to my permanent-duty station, a buddy and I went in together on a restaurant. Nothing fancy, just a good solid lunch place that served Korean food. It had a good location and it did well. When I got out, it had two other locations and was turning into a small chain. My buddy bought me out. With what I put away and the buyout, I had about five years or so to figure out what I wanted to do. Thought about going private, but I'd worked with contractors before and I didn't like it. Something rubs me the wrong way about the soldier-for-hire gig. I'd been through Texas a few times, and I enjoyed it. So I picked a small town, bought a decent house, and tried being a civilian to see how long I would last. And then some alien piece of shit came into my territory and started killing dogs and people, so here we are."

That was the longest I've ever heard him speak. It must've been rough to keep looking and looking and never finding that right spot, that place that said home.

"Even a generation later, with all the opportunities in the world, still a soldier. The genetic programming held in the next generation." Wilmos studied him. "They didn't tell you about Auul?"

Sean shook his head.

Wilmos sighed. "I can't say I blame them."

He turned to me.

"Are those Anansi pearls in your cart?"

"Yes."

"What are you going up against?"

"A dahaka," I said. Why not? Maybe he knew something about it.

"A nasty breed. Need all the ammunition you can get."

He glanced at Sean. Sean was looking at the corner again, at the scale armor.

"Why don't you take a closer look?" Wilmos said.

Sean rose and walked over to the armor. "What is it?"

"Auroon Twelve. Stealth armor, made specifically for alphas."

"It looks..." I searched for the right word.

"Flimsy?" Wilmos nodded. "It's nano armor. Meant to fit under your skin. Once you put it on, it never comes off. Every alpha wore some version of it. They used to say you don't wear the armor, the armor wears you. It's designed to change with your body, any form, any shape. Ever seen your mother or your father show tattoos on their necks when they're upset?"

Sean nodded. "Sure."

"Then you know when the tattoos show, you're in trouble. It's an instinctual response. When you're angry or threatened, the armor expands to cover vulnerable areas. It's calling you, isn't it?"

"Yes," Sean said.

"Is it for sale?" I asked.

"No. But it can be had." Wilmos smiled at Sean. "If you want it, it's yours. I have no use for it. But sometime in the future I might call on you for a favor, alpha. That time may come never or tomorrow."

Sean thought about it.

"Take it," Wilmos said. "It's a good trade."

"No. It's a bad idea." I knew he would never take it. Not in a million years He didn't trust Wilmos and it was a sucker's deal...

Sean held out his hand. "You've got a deal."

Wilmos shook it. "Good. Take your shirt off. We'll get it fitted."

"Sean...," I said.

He looked at me. "I don't know why, but I have to have it. I can't stop myself."

"It's a built-in compulsion," Wilson said. "Don't worry. Once it's on, the feeling will pass."

"If it's a compulsion, it might not be a good idea," I told him.

"I know." Sean's eyes were open wide, his pupils so large that his irises looked completely black.

"It will be useful to you. I promise," Wilmos said. "You'll feel better."

He turned off the force field. Sean stepped forward, pulled off his shirt, and touched the shiny scales. The metal melted, wrapping around his fingers. Thin streaks of gray slid around his arm like metal snakes, over his shoulders, over his chest... The metal expanded, coating him, and broke apart into a thousand tiny metal dots. For a second nothing happened, then the dots moved as one, piercing Sean's skin.

He screamed, a guttural, brutal shout that turned into a roar.

His back arched, his shoulders gaining bulk. His flesh whipped around him in a furry whirlwind and a huge werewolf stood in Sean's place. I had forgotten how big he was.

Wilmos blinked. "That's one hell of a wetwork shape."

Werewolf-Sean growled, displaying huge teeth.

"Feel the armor move through you," Wilmos said. "Let it bond. It will make you stronger. You should feel some feedback right away, but the complete merger will take time. Give it twenty-four hours and it will be in your bones."

Sean turned. Armored plates formed under his skin on his chest, guarding his pectorals and the flat ridges of his stomach. The armor melted and the bulk of it shifted to his shoulders, forming pauldrons. His neck thickened. He snarled. The fur vanished, his body slimmed down in a blink, and human Sean was back. Swirls of dark blue-gray pigment crisscrossed his chest and stomach like tiger stripes. He looked down at himself. The pigment moved.

"That's it," Wilmos said. "Shape it."

The pigment melted and turned into a tribal design that covered most of Sean's torso. It wrapped around his ribs, flowed onto his back, and settled.

Sean exhaled.

"And now you're ready for battle. Good luck, soldier."

CHAPTER SIXTEEN

When we came back, Arland was waiting for us in the kitchen. He'd found the guest laptop I'd left in the room for his convenience and was reading something on the screen. A cup of tea with small roses on it sat next to him. The air smelled like mint. Even in a white T-shirt and jeans, Arland didn't fit into the kitchen. It was like walking into your room and finding a medieval knight with the face of a superstar casually sipping tea from your flowery porcelain cup.

The vampire saw Sean. His eyes narrowed. "Did something happen?"

"No," Sean told him.

Arland studied him. "You look different. You look larger." He inhaled. "And your scent has changed. Something did happen."

Something happened all right. Sean hadn't said a word after we left the shop. He did look larger, better defined, as if he'd gained about ten pounds of muscle and it all went to the right places. His eyes, more golden than amber now, looked into the distance. He was wandering somewhere inside his head, and antagonizing him right now wasn't wise. Somehow I didn't think that he'd respond with werewolf poetry. He kept shrugging his shoulders as if he wanted to test them out.

"What are you reading?" I asked.

"Just some minor social research," Arland said.

Okay. "Did the battlefield meet with your approval?"

"It will suffice. Have you acquired your weapons?"

"Yes," I said.

"I'm going to go for a run." Sean opened the back door and went outside.

I moved to the window. He was standing in the grass, looking up at the sky.

Arland's eyebrows crept together. "Should I be concerned?"

"Probably not." I had no idea. I was concerned. In my book, putting on alien suits that bonded with your body wasn't wise. But Sean was a grown man, and there wasn't anything I could've done about it. I had no idea what side effects this stunt could have.

Sean shrugged his shoulders again and took off, dashing into the trees. A moment and he vanished completely from view.

Here's hoping he came back in one piece.

"Lady Dina," Arland said.

I turned to him. "Dina, please."

"Dina." Arland leaned back and presented me with a dazzling smile, his fangs on display.

Uh-oh. Perhaps keeping "lady" in front of my name would've been a better strategy.

He rose and walked over to me. I used to read an action series about a former military detective who was almost six and a half feet tall. I'd never quite comprehended how tall that was, but Arland had just given me a very good idea.

"Do you need to make any preparations?" Arland stopped next to me and leaned his forearm against the wall, looking out of the window. "If so, how long they will take?"

"About seven hours, give or take a few minutes depending on temperature," I said. That was the average time it took the pearls to mature once planted.

"Will you be comfortable with fighting tonight?" he asked.

"Yes." This was the weirdest conversation.

Arland nodded. "Dina..."

"Yes?"

"This entire affair has many components in it. Pride, revenge, betrayal... All very important." He turned and looked at me with his dark blue eyes. "I'm honor and duty bound to resolve this. The future of my House depends on it. I don't know what Sean's motivations are beyond territoriality, and I don't know if I can rely on him. But no matter what my commitments are, I will promise you this: your safety is my first priority. I wish you had chosen to remain behind."

"Because I'm a woman?" I asked quietly.

"Because you will be the only person in the fight who hasn't been trained as a killer. I have seen my mother and my grandmother on the battlefield. Any vampire with half a mind knows better than to stand between a woman and her chosen target. When a man takes up arms, he does so for many reasons. Sometimes to punish, sometimes to intimidate or frighten. But when a woman picks up a weapon, she means to kill. So please do not take this as an insult."

He leaned toward me. Suddenly the space between us shrank.

"I will do everything in my power to ensure your survival, and should the need arise, I will put myself between danger and you." His voice was quiet and intimate. "Do not hesitate to use me as your shield."

His voice sent tiny shivers through me.

Wow. He was something else.

Arland smiled again, showing me his fangs. Vampires smiled for many reasons, but when a vampire male smiled at you from this distance with that kind of look in his eyes, it was done for one purpose only: to impress. *Look at my big teeth. I'm an apex predator. My genetic material is awesome.*

I had to say something. "I'll keep that in mind. Now if you excuse me, I have some preparations to make."

I picked up my broom, went outside, pulled the cart out with my magic, stuck the broom into it, and started toward the clearing. The cart rolled behind me.

No, this wouldn't do. I had to keep at least some semblance of normality and I was getting sloppy. Appearing normal even when nobody who mattered could see us was how innkeepers had kept up our disguises for so long. I sighed, circled the cart, and put my hands on the handles.

Vampires have been hitting on me since I was about fifteen. Mostly vampire boys. Vampires, as a species, lived to conquer. Their cultural identity was wrapped up around challenges, and both male and female vampires went after their targets with single-minded precision. As the daughter of innkeepers, I was off-limits and therefore irresistible. Nothing had ever come of it, and I was used to it by now, but something about Arland, the way he looked at me, or the way he smiled, sent a shiver of alarm through me. It wasn't unpleasant, which was troubling. Being involved with the Marshal of a Holy Anocracy House wasn't on my agenda. They didn't do "involved." They only did total and complete victory. I had to nip this in the bud.

Where could Sean have gotten off to? If that suit had strangled him and he now lay dying somewhere, I wouldn't even know. Idiot werewolf.

I reached the edge of clearing. Here the short, stocky trees parted to encircle a clear field. The boundary of the inn ended about twelve feet ahead. I took the broom from the cart, turned it into a narrow shovel, and thrust it into the ground. The hole grew around it, wider, deeper...

Little more.

Hmm. About a foot deep should do it.

Okay, good enough. Now I just had to make thirty-one more.

I turned and almost walked into Sean. His face was slicked with a faint sheen of sweat. His cloak was gone. He wore a T-shirt that left his arms bare, and the same damp sheen covered the carved muscle of his biceps. He stared at my face, his eyes so light they almost glowed. I looked into them and saw the wolf looking right back at me.

Every cell in my body went on full alert. My broom sprouted a blade.

Sean smiled, a feral grin like a wolf panting. "Dina." He practically purred.

"Are you okay?"

He glanced at my broom, amused. "What are you doing here, all alone?"

This was reminding me of Red Riding Hood. If he asked what was in my basket, he would regret it. "I'm not alone. I have my broom."

He leaned forward, closing the six inches between us. The dark tattoo designs slid up and down his neck and chest. The wolf in his eyes beckoned.

Oh no. No, no, no. We were not going there, into those dark woods.

I touched the tip of my spear to the underside of his chin. The heat coming off his skin warmed my hand.

"Ooh." He wrinkled his nose at me. "Sharp."

"I think your new outfit got you a little too excited." I began to pool the magic under him.

"I'm going to kiss you," he said.

"What?"

He pushed my spear aside with his fingers and bent down. His hand slid into my hair. His mouth closed on mine.

Kissing Sean Evans was like drinking a shot of the strongest liquor in the world while it was on fire.

His tongue touched my lips, stroking, teasing, not attacking but seducing; confident but subtle. Excitement shot through me like an electric shock and some sort of vital switch in my brain malfunctioned, fried by the burst of need. I opened my mouth and let him in, our bodies perfectly in tune. He wanted me and I kissed him back.

We broke apart. My body was hot, my head was dizzy. The wolf eyes laughed at me. He looked like he was about to repeat that kiss.

Sean leaned forward.

I pushed. The ground under him yawned and he sank into it up to his hips.

He grinned. "Was it that good for you?"

I dropped him another eighteen inches.

Sean laughed.

"You're interfering with my work. Don't make me bury you."

"If you bury me, you'll have to dig me up for the fight."

"Maybe I'll just leave you in the ground."

I made another hole, took a pearl, which was about the size of a honeydew melon, from the cart, and slid it into the soil.

"Why?" he asked.

"You'll see tonight." I made another hole and planted the next pearl in it. "That suit has gone to your head."

"It's not the suit, buttercup."

"I don't do pet names."

"Do you do werewolves?"

"Okay, I'm not talking to you anymore. I'm going to plant the rest of these, and if you stay very quiet, I might find a drop of compassion in my heart and dig you out before you sprout roots."

He grinned and strained. Muscles bulged on his chest.

"Very impressive, but –"

Sean shot out of the hole and took off into the trees.

Whoa.

I tracked him with my magic. He was running like a madman, bouncing up and down off the tree trunks.

First Arland, now him. Was it something in the air? Maybe fighting the dahaka had gotten them all excited. I didn't know and quite frankly I didn't care. I wanted to kill the dahaka and send both of them home.

Dahaka… Thinking about the fight opened this gaping hole in my stomach that refused to close. Maybe the two of them thought they were going to die and this was their chance to go out strong. I really hoped not.

It was a nice kiss. Very… memorable.

If he came near me with that look again, I'd hit him upside the head and claim self-defense. No jury in the world would convict me.

The day slowly burned down to evening. I had set the kitchen timer and it told me it'd been exactly six hours and thirty-five minutes since I planted the pearls. They would hatch in nineteen minutes.

In the foyer Arland sat on the loveseat, sipping mint tea. The vampire wore a full set of armor; the breastplate and the raised pauldrons made his shoulders and chest appear enormous. His weapon, a giant blood mace, lay next to him on the floor, its head solid black and crossed by glowing red lines.

Sean sat across from him in a chair, Beast curled by his feet. Sean wore sweatpants and a dark shirt. His bare feet rested on the floorboards. He planned to go into wetwork shape and he said boots hindered his mobility. Two large machetes rested next to him. Well, one was a machete. The other looked like a hybrid of a gladius and an oversized bowie knife.

"So crosses don't do anything against your kind?" Sean asked.

"No," Arland said. "There is no mystical force repelling us."

"Then why?"

"We're forbidden to kill a creature in a moment of prayer or invocation of their deity. Well, we can, technically, but you have to do penance and purify yourself and nobody wants to spend weeks praying and bathing themselves in the sacred cave springs. The water's only a fraction warmer than ice. When one of you holds up a cross, it's difficult to determine whether you're praying, invoking, or just waving it around. So the sane strategy is to back away."

"What about garlic?"

"That comes from gravediggers," I told him. "When they exhumed bodies, they would wear garlands of garlic to keep from gagging."

"Holy water?" Sean asked.

"That charming practice originated in Byzantium," Arland said. "Your churches stored a lot of gold, so to keep the undesirables away, the priests would keep quicklime powder on hand. We're positive there were other ingredients in the powder as well, but quicklime was present in abundance. They'd toss a handful of quicklime in your face and dump holy water on you. The water reacts with quicklime, igniting and turning extremely corrosive. But no, I've dipped my hand in your blessed water before and by itself, it does absolutely nothing."

"Where did you get the holy water?" I asked.

"My cousin brought it as a souvenir. I did it on a dare. Logically, of course, I knew it wouldn't melt my skin off, but one can never be certain."

I pictured a bunch of teenage vampires standing around a basin. *"You touch it." "No, you touch it..."* Of course, he would put his hand into it.

My timer went off.

"Is it that time?" Sean asked.

I nodded and petted Beast one last time. "Guard the house. Stay inside."

Beast whined softly. I didn't want me to go either, but I had no choice about it.

We went out the door. Sean carried a blade in each hand. Arland carried his mace. I carried my broom. The sun had set, but its wake still diluted the sky's purple to pale yellow in the west. The moon rose, bright, huge, like a silver coin in the sky. The scent of grass and the weak aroma of burning wood from someone's fire pit swirled around me. Noises came in clear: the faint sound of our feet, the distant barking of a dog, a siren somewhere far away... The world seemed so sharp somehow. I was wearing jeans during a Texas summer evening, and still I felt cold.

I really didn't want to die.

"Fear is good," Sean told me.

"Too much fear isn't good," Arland said. "Don't worry, I'll be there."

Sean put his hand on my arm and stopped, letting Arland go forward a few steps. He leaned to me and said quietly, "Don't count on him or on me. If things don't go well, you turn around, run back to the house, and let the inn guns blow that bastard to pieces if he follows. I left my parents' number on your kitchen table. Call them if something happens. They'll help."

Two thoughts occurred at the same time. One said "If I could get the dahaka on the grounds, I wouldn't need the guns" and the second said "He's worried enough to do this for me." That last one cut right through the fear of impending death and freaked me right the heck out.

There was no way on Earth I could be falling for Sean Evans. The list of his shortcomings was a mile long: arrogant, unstable, bossy, werewolf... who'd saved me from dying in a Costco parking lot and who kissed like... I shut my brain off and made my lips move. "Thank you."

Sean nodded.

We came to the edge of the field. The Anansi pearls had grown and broken through the soil, rising a few inches above the dirt like the tops of giant mushrooms about to break free. Each of them should be the size of a small tire now, but with most of their bulk buried it was hard to tell. I hoped they were done. Sometimes there were some minor variations due to temperature. The only way to know for sure would be to break one, but once broken, they wouldn't last long in Earth's atmosphere.

Sean stared at the pearls.

Arland raised his eyebrows.

"You sure about this?" Sean asked me.

"Yes. My father's used them before."

Sean and Arland walked out into the field. Although it was technically my property, the inn wasn't yet strong enough to claim it. The grounds ended at the field's edge. I sighed and followed the two men. The protective mantle of magic slid off me. I felt naked.

Arland took out his crest. His fingers danced over the surface. "It's done. It's broadcasting the signal of the person I think betrayed us. The dahaka will show up soon."

"Let's hope you're right," I said.

A minute passed. Another. Time slowed to a crawl. Funny how long a minute can last. If you're reading a good book, it flies by. If you're holding your breath, it moves slower than a snail.

"What if he doesn't show?" I asked.

"He'll show," Sean said. "He wants to get paid."

"And once he sees us, it will be a challenge," Arland said.

We stood shoulder to shoulder. "Shouldn't we have set some traps?" I asked.

"He's too mobile," Arland said. "He'd avoid whatever we set up and we'd stumble into our defenses in the fight. Besides, we are the trap."

He and Sean had planted an energy disruptor a few hours ago. According to Arland, it would negate whatever energy weapons the dahaka carried, and apparently, dahakas didn't care for projectile technology.

Sean raised his face to the moon and inhaled. His ears twitched. "Incoming. About two miles out." He glanced at me. "Dina, remember, stick to the plan, no matter how hard it is. It's a good plan and it will work."

A shiver ran down his spine, like fire down a detonator cord. His skin split. Mist swirled around him. For a long moment his face remained human and then it too burst, bones growing, flesh stretching. His back expanded, layered with thick, hard muscle. He raised his new massive arms, which were covered with gray fur, and held them out. The armor burst out of his pores, sheathing the body in a tight dark sleeve. Reinforced plates formed over his abdomen. Flexible darkness covered his massive neck. He pulled his clothes off, ripping them off almost as an afterthought.

The armor sheathed him, dark like tar, but unlike glossy tar, it swallowed the moonlight. The black turned, twisted, lightened, and a pattern of gray and blue formed on its surface, matching the trees and the grass so exactly he became practically invisible.

"Try to keep him still," Sean-wolf growled.

"Worry about yourself," Arland said.

Sean nodded, sprinted across the clearing, and jumped up, scrambling up the tree. His armor shifted, adjusting, and I could no longer see him.

A low, murmuring growl, like a dozen voices speaking at once, rolled through the trees. The stalkers were coming.

"Just like we rehearsed," Arland said and walked over to the side.

"I remember," I told him.

Pale eyes ignited at the other end of the clearing. Thin shapes dashed through the trees.

"No fear," Arland said.

One says be afraid, the other says don't be afraid. Perfect.

The first stalker emerged into the moonlight, an ugly, alien thing. It sniffed the air tentatively and looked at me.

Arland stood perfectly still.

More stalkers joined the first, condensing from the twilight. Wow. I hadn't expected this many. Alarm squirmed through me.

The lead stalker dipped his head, unsure. Behind the horde, a dark shape rose, taller and standing on two legs. The dahaka.

Stalkers were predators. Like dogs, like cats, like bears, they all reacted to the same behavior. It was an instinctual reaction and we were counting on it.

I turned and ran.

The growls behind me raised the hair on the back of my neck, whipping me into a frenzy. I dashed across the field. The noise behind me swelled. They chased me.

I shot through the inn's boundary, sending the magic in front of me in a wide fan. The tops of the Anansi pearls cracked in unison.

I spun around, the broom in my hand shifting into a halberd.

More than half the stalkers ran across the field in a ragged wave, ignoring Arland. The rest lingered at the edge of the field.

The dahaka strode out of the trees. If he called them back now, it was all over. Both Arland and Sean didn't think he would —he would want to take me out before I reached the inn and turned its defenses on him.

Red lines ignited in Arland's armor. The blood mace whined, priming.

The dahaka roared, the remaining stalkers echoing his voice.

Arland snarled back, a harsh, primal challenge.

The stalkers were almost on me.

The tops of the pearls pulsated. Please be ripe, please be ripe...

Arland trotted forward like a tank that was trying to build up speed.

The first stalker crossed the boundary. I let it come.

It leaped at me. I spun my halberd and sliced across its ribs. White blood flew. The stalkers howled in unison and sped up. That's right. Come closer.

The injured stalker whirled and fell as tree roots wrapped around his body and throat.

Beyond the mass of stalkers, the dahaka charged out of the trees and struck at Arland.

The stalkers mobbed me. I cut the first, then the second, spinning the halberd around me, playing for time. Claws carved my leg. Someone ripped at my back. Now.

The ground gave under the stalkers, sucking them in. It wouldn't hold but for a few seconds. That would have to be enough.

The tops of the Anansi pearls burst. Spiders as big as my fist, their backs glowing with electric green, poured out of the eggs. They swarmed the stalkers. Their jaws punctured flesh, injecting lethal poison. The stalkers screeched in unison as their tissue began to liquefy.

In the field, Arland and the dahaka clashed. The alien dwarfed the vampire, towering a full foot above Arland's head. Arland wasn't slow, but the dahaka was so fast. He snarled, turning back and forth, slicing at Arland with a short blue blade. The blows rained on the vampire, but he stood his ground. The stalkers snapped and lunged at him, their claws sliding off his armor.

A chunk of Arland's armor fell to the ground, wet with blood.

The vampire grunted, teeth bared. His mace connected with the dahaka's shoulder. The impact threw the dahaka back. He stumbled, then charged again. Arland braced himself. The alien turned, whipping his massive tail. It smashed into Arland, staggering him to the side.

"Faster," I whispered to the Anansi's children. "Kill faster."

They didn't understand my word, but they understood my tone. The spiders fed faster, gorging themselves. The stalkers inside the inn boundary convulsed, moaning. There was nothing I could do until the stalkers were dead. Both Sean and Arland had stressed to me that this was my part of the plan and it was essential I killed them all.

Another chunk of armor flew from Arland. The dahaka was carving him out of it, piece by piece.

Where the hell was Sean? Come on. He wouldn't chicken out. He just couldn't.

Arland took another tail hit on the side. His head hung. He shook it slowly, as if dazed.

"Faster," I pushed the spiders. If I moved without them, I'd lose control of the swarm. They would live just long enough to fill the Avalon Subdivision with the lifeless husks of its former inhabitants. "Hurry."

The dahaka spun around the vampire like a bladed whirlwind. Blood drenched Arland's armor. He gasped. The dahaka sliced across the back of his legs. Arland went down on one knee.

The largest of the spiders fell on its side. Its legs jerked spasmodically and became still. I had pushed them too far too fast. Damn it.

The last stalker wailed and died.

I strode across the boundary and the rest of the spiders followed me, intoxicated by my magic. Behind me the last of the stalkers sank softly to the ground, dry shells of their formerly impressive selves.

The dahaka barked a short command. The remaining stalkers charged at me.

The alien swung his blade, aiming for Arland's bowed head.

I ran. The spiders surged forward, heading for the alien, and washed over the remaining stalkers.

Three things happened at once: the dahaka struck, bringing his blade down; Arland spun out of the way; and a lean shadow appeared behind the dahaka as if by magic and sank a sword into his spine.

The alien screamed. Sean sliced at him, cutting and slashing with his swords. The dahaka counterattacked with fast, brutal cuts, but Sean was too fast. The assassin's sword whistled through the air, cutting nothing.

The two spiders by my feet cringed and fell over. One by one, my spider horde began to die.

Arland rose to his feet, suddenly fast and limber, and smashed the dahaka's side with his mace. Together the werewolf and the vampire began pushing the dahaka. The blood mace whirred and struck home and for every blow of Arland's weapon, Sean landed two or three cuts. The dahaka fought back with vicious fury. Blood sprayed, and I no longer could tell whose. They kept pressing him, driving him across the clearing toward me.

He should've been disabled by now. That was the plan. But he danced back and forth, fully mobile. At any moment, he could break away and run, and we would have to chase him. Neither Arland nor I would be fast enough. The dahaka was outnumbered and wounded. He was losing and he knew it. I could feel him teetering on the brink of a decision. If he ran, it would be all over.

I melted my halberd in a bundle of blue filaments. It spiraled around my hands and waist, extending to sink deep into the ground behind me. I sent my magic down through it. My power streamed from me like electric current through the wire and back into the inn, forging a connection.

I cried out. It was a small, scared noise.

The dahaka spun and saw me, standing alone and weaponless outside the inn's boundary, my spiders dead around me. The purple eyes gleamed. In the split second he stared at me, I saw the calculation plain in those alien eyes. Sean pressed him from one side and Arland from the other. I was the only possible exit. He could maim me in passing or grab me and use me as a hostage, and either way the two men would abandon their pursuit and concentrate on helping me. It was a win-win scenario.

The dahaka whipped around and charged at me.

Sean chased him, but the alien moved too fast.

I stood still. My heart was pounding too fast to count. Blood thudded through my head. The air tasted like metal.

The dahaka came toward me, fast, unstoppable, like a train flying off the rails.

I spread my arms and leaned forward, bringing them together, my fingers reaching for him. All of my power, everything that made me an innkeeper, moved with me. Behind me the house creaked, mimicking my movement. Every tree branch, every blade of grass, and every stray root reached forward with me. Wind bathed the dahaka like the breath of a giant clearing his lungs just before he inhaled. The alien realized it was a trap and spun around in a desperate rush to get away. Sean cut at him, but the alien batted him aside. For a second the way to his escape looked clear, and then Arland drove his massive shoulder into the dahaka, knocking him back toward me.

I straightened and pulled the empty air with both hands. The wind roared as the entire inn pulled with me. The dahaka howled, straining to resist the storm made just for him. His feet sank into the soil. He dropped down to all fours, clawing at the dirt, screeching in pure terror.

The house and I pulled, trying to drag him into the inn.

The dahaka slid across the grass, straight to me. Somehow he flipped and leaped straight up at me, claws out, teeth bared. Filaments bristled like narrow javelins and shot from me, piercing him in a dozen places. The dahaka howled, suspended in midair, flailing like a fish on a hook. Behind him, Sean leaped ten feet up and severed the dahaka's head with one precise blow.

It rolled to my feet. The purple fire went out of the alien's eyes.

My knees buckled and I sat on the grass. It reached to me, rubbing against me like a cat arching its back, eager for a stroke.

We'd won.

Sean sat on the grass next to me. Blood slicked his skin. The dahaka had gotten in a few good cuts.

We watched as Arland searched the dahaka's armor. He found something, examined it closely, and came to sit next to us. In his hands was a vampire's crest. He showed it to me. "I activated it and sent a message. He's coming."

"He?" Sean asked.

"My cousin."

"How did you know?" Sean asked.

"He'd opposed the Pact of Brotherhood. Nothing forceful, just a snide comment here and there, enough to let us know he wasn't happy about it. Orig has poor impulse control. As a child, he got into fights for frivolous reasons. As an adolescent, he had to learn the hard way that women don't enjoy being assaulted. He is at his best when he is set loose on the battlefield in the ranks, but in his mind, he is the Marshal. He spoke at the feast in my aunt's honor after we buried her. It was all outrage and bluster and how we would find those responsible and make them regret ever crawling out of their mother's womb. After the funeral I saw him standing by himself. I was above him on the terrace and he thought he was alone. He was smiling. I thought it was odd at the time. I used your terminal to check with the House. They pulled his flight plans for the past six months. A month before the wedding, he'd taken a trip to Savva. The idiot had charged the House for the fuel. There is one in every family."

Sean glanced at me.

"Savva is the mercenary capital of the galaxy," I told him. "If you wanted to hire a killer, that would be the place."

Arland grimaced. "Now I'll have to mop up his mess."

"Now?" I asked.

He nodded. "I want to get this over with."

"Don't you want to heal up?" I asked.

"No, I don't." The way he said it made it clear he wanted the questions dropped.

We sat together, bleeding quietly onto the grass. I hurt in half a dozen places. Funny how in the fight I hadn't noticed, but apparently, I was all cut up to hell. The inn could heal the magical injuries but not the physical ones. Well, this would cure me of looking for trouble for at least a few weeks.

The screen door clanged. I turned around. Lord Soren, out of his armor and limping, struggled forth. He crossed the property and lowered himself on the grass next to Arland.

Arland nodded to him. "Is there a precedent for outsiders serving as witnesses?"

"Yes," Lord Soren said.

"Good."

The sky above us split. A bright red orb formed in the air and drained down in a silent, glowing waterfall of red, leaving three new vampires on the grass. The tallest looked a lot like Arland. If they were human, I'd say the cousin was about six or seven years older, but with vampires, nobody could tell.

Arland rose and walked over. "Why?"

The vampire snarled back.

"Engage your translator," Arland said. "My witnesses don't speak our language."

I leaned over to Lord Soren. "Orig isn't your son, is he?" Because that would be awful.

"No," the older vampire said. "Other side of the family."

Orig fixed Arland with a glowing stare. "This alliance, this brotherhood you and your father dragged us into. It's not good for anyone. We've had two years of peace. Two years of no raids, no challenges, and no glory. We're going soft and stale. You don't care, and I get that you don't care. You have achieved your place, but the rest of us are not as lucky. Not everyone can be the golden son. Some of us have ranks to climb."

"You had the exact same opportunities I did," Arland said. "You didn't rise through the ranks because you're an undisciplined idiot. You want to know my secret? Before you earn the right to give orders, you have to follow them. We were going to launch a joint offensive against House Lon this fall. It would've been massive and it would let us extend our influence over the entire continent. The offensive is now dead. Congratulations, Orig. You single-handedly crushed three years of planning. You brought in an outsider to assassinate your own aunt, and you've permitted him to soil your crest. It will be years before we can wipe away the stench of your foul stain from our name."

"And if I want a trial?" Orig asked.

Arland dropped his gauntlets on the grass. His breast-plate followed. "You get a trial right here. You're not going back to the House to grandstand and posture. I'm the Marshal of House Krahr. I've conducted my investigation. Here, before these witnesses, I find you guilty of treason. Defend yourself."

Orig bared his teeth. The armor fell off him. "I will bury you on this planet."

"Big words. Just try to die well. Don't shame the House any further."

They clashed. No weapons, just bare hands and teeth. It was short and brutal. I really wanted to close my eyes a couple of times, but I was a witness and so I watched until Arland bit through the back of his cousin's neck. He shook his prey once like a dog shakes a rat and spat him out.

"Remove this filth."

The two vampires who had arrived with Orig collected his body. Lord Soren lumbered to his feet and followed them. Arland wiped the blood from his lips.

"Aren't you going with them?" Sean asked.

"I thought I would impose on you for just a little while longer," Arland said to me. "I really would like to shower. And to brush my teeth. I need to get the taste of family out of my mouth."

I was sitting in the foyer, trying to read a novel about angels and women who fell in love with them. The novel was great, but I couldn't sink into it. I had showered and made myself some chamomile tea, but sleeping seemed impossible.

This had been my first major clash in my own inn. I'd won, but somehow I didn't feel triumphant. I felt... spent.

Sean emerged from the kitchen and set a cup of coffee in front of me. He'd washed the blood off his face. "Hey."

"Hey," I said.

"So what's next for you?" he asked.

"Next I go on as usual," I said. "The Innkeeper Assembly may send someone to investigate, but I can hold them off. What's next for you?"

"I owe a favor to Wilmos," Sean said.

No. Suddenly I realized what was coming.

He looked at his coffee. "I'm pretty sure I know what kind of favor he wants. I thought I'd go and pay him back before he thinks something up. I'd like to see what's out there. I'd like to see Savva. Other places. You know."

I knew. I could see it in his eyes. I'd had the same look once, that exciting knowledge that somewhere just beyond the space horizon, something secret and exciting waited for you. Something you'd never seen before and probably would never see again. He'd always been looking for the place he belonged. The lure of the unknown was irresistible. "You're leaving."

"Not forever," he said. "I want to work off my debt to Wilmos. When someone mentions some planet or some gadget, I don't want to be the only one in the room who doesn't know what it is. I feel like I blundered through this thing with my eyes half shut. I want to open them and see."

Something inside me dropped. I hadn't realized how much I liked him and now he was leaving.

I could ask him to stay. He might even do it. He liked me. At least I thought he did. But he wouldn't be happy and it wouldn't last for long. The Great Beyond was calling. I knew how strong that pull was. I'd answered it and wandered around the cosmos for years before coming finally home. Time wasn't always the same there as it was here.

The words came out slowly. "The galaxy is very large. It lured away my brother. Klaus is still somewhere out there." I pointed up. "I haven't heard from him in forever. Don't be like my brother, Sean. Keep in touch."

"I'll try."

"Do you need me to open a door for you?"

Sean shook his head. "Wilmos gave me a gadget. One-way transportation to Baha-char."

"It's easy to get lost there. Be careful."

"I will," he said.

Arland descended the stairs. He was freshly showered. "I thought to stay longer, but it seems the House won't let me. I have settled my account, Lady Dina. My uncle and I were most pleased with our stay and your discretion."

Everybody was leaving. That was a fact of the innkeeper's life: guests left. New guests would arrive. I had just made a mistake of being too involved with one of them. I wouldn't repeat it next time. "Thank you."

Arland knelt by me. "I have to go, but I will return. And when I do, I hope you will grant me the privilege of staying at your inn."

"You're welcome any time, Lord Arland."

He hesitated. "I don't suppose you would join me…"

"I wouldn't. Not at this time. I belong at the inn."

He nodded. "I reserve the right to try to change your mind."

I forced a smile.

Arland walked out the door.

Sean halted. "Do I get a good-bye kiss?"

"It will just make things harder, Sean. You chose your road. You should follow it and not look back."

He opened his mouth as if to say something, turned, and walked out. I flicked my fingers. "Terminal, please." A flat screen formed on the wall and I watched them head to the orchard. The sun was rising. They had to hurry.

The inn was safe. I had done my job. All was well.

All was well.

"What are you intentions toward Dina?" Arland asked on the screen.

"My intentions are my business," Sean said.

"Mhm," Arland said. "I have spent my spare time studying literature popular with young women of this planet. One should always study the battlefield."

Sean glanced at him. "And?"

"I suggest you give up now. According to my research, in a vampire-werewolf love triangle, the vampire always gets the girl."

"Is that so?" Sean asked.

"It is."

"In that case, may the best man win."

Arland considered it and grinned. "I can live with that."

The red glow claimed him and he vanished, sucked upward.

Sean stopped. The orchard stretched in front of him. He took something out of his pocket. Reality tore in front of him like a plastic bag pulled apart. A narrow gap formed between the trees and through it I saw the familiar busy street. Wilmos' shop shimmered in the distance.

Sean took a deep breath and stepped into the gap.

EPILOGUE

The phone rang. I looked up from my novel. Beast raised her head from her spot on the rug by my legs. Gertrude Hunt wasn't listed in any of the normal hotel directories. We had no website and no listed number in the yellow pages. Normally a ringing phone would be unusual, except somehow my number had gotten on to a political polls company's hit list and no amount of telling them that I was on a Do Not Call list could convince them to stop.

Another ring. I'd spent most of the day reading and drinking tea, trying to recuperate with mixed results and I didn't feel like getting up.

Another ring. Fine.

I crawled out of my chair and walked to the phone. If they asked me one more time if I approved of my congressman, I would use my powers for evil.

"Gertrude Hunt," I said into the phone.

"Dina," Mr. Rodriguez said. "How are you?"

"I'm well, thank you."

"Congratulations on taking care of your problem."

"How did you know?"

Mr. Rodriguez chuckled. "Check your mailbox."

I listened to the disconnect signal. Hmm.

I glanced at Beast. "Should we?"

She jumped up and made a circle around my feet.

I walked outside, through the heat of the afternoon, and opened my mailbox. Junk mail, pizza flyer... and a small padded envelope from Mr. Rodriguez. I pried it open and slid out a small brochure. The cover, printed in black on plain white paper said "Directory."

I knew exactly what it was. It was the listing of all of the inns issued by the Innkeeper Assembly. I opened the front page and turned to News and Changes. A single item was circled in ballpoint pen.

House Krahr of Holy Cosmic Anocracy has made it known that all inquiries regarding its members in North America are to be addressed to Gertrude Hunt Inn. This announcement comes on the heels of Wilmos Gerwar of Baha-char's endorsement of the same inn.

The words Gertrude Hunt had two and a half stars next to them.

I leaned against the oak. I had earned a half star. I could barely believe it.

In the margin of the page Mr. Rodriguez had written, "Your parents would be so proud."

I looked at the sky. They were out there somewhere.

"I'm on my way," I whispered. "Wait for me. I will find you, I promise."

The End

11303005R00133

Made in the USA
San Bernardino, CA
12 May 2014